William—The Showman

also published by
Macmillan Children's Books

"DAD'S A DENTIST," SAID THE GIRL. "AND IF YOU HANG ABOUT
OUR GATE HE'LL COME AND PULL OUT YOUR TEETH FOR YOU."

(See page 52)

William—The Showman

RICHMAL CROMPTON

Illustrated by Thomas Henry

MACMILLAN CHILDREN'S BOOKS

First published 1937

Copyright Richmal C. Ashbee

The illustrations by Thomas Henry are reproduced
by permission of the Hamlyn Group Picture Library

First published in this edition 1986 by

MACMILLAN CHILDREN'S BOOKS
A division of Macmillan Publishers Limited
London and Basingstoke
Associated companies throughout the world

Reprinted 1988

British Library Cataloguing in Publication Data
Crompton, Richmal
William the showman.
Rn: Richmal Crompton Lamburn I. Title
823'.912[J] PZ7

ISBN 0-333-42615-0
ISBN 0-333-42616-9 Pbk

Phototypeset by Wyvern Typesetting Ltd, Bristol
Printed in Hong Kong

Contents

An invitation from William

Join my club and becum a nOutlaw
William Brown

You can join the Outlaws Club!
You will receive
✳ **a special Outlaws wallet containing**
your own Outlaws badge
the Club Rules
and
a letter from William giving you the secret password

To join the Club send a letter with your name and address written in block capitals telling us you want to join the Outlaws, and a postal order for 45p, to

The Outlaws Club
577 Kingston Road
Raynes Park
LONDON SW20 8SA

You must live in the United Kingdom or the Republic of Ireland in order to join.

Chapter 1

William and the Sea-side Show

"WE'RE not goin' to the sea-side this year," announced William.

"Nor us," said Ginger.

"Nor us," said Douglas.

"Nor us," said Henry.

"Seems silly to me," said William after a slight pause, "that the sea-side should only be at the sea. Seems to me that if only people'd take a bit of trouble they could have it anywhere."

"How could they?" challenged Ginger.

"Well, there mus' be some way," said William. "There's some way of doin' everythin' if only you can think of it. How d'you think people'd have invented electricity an' motors an' potato peelers an' things if there hadn't been?"

"But there's got to be *sea* at the sea-side," said Douglas. "You can't have sea-side anywhere but at the sea."

"Well, what's the sea but water?" replied William. "An' you can have water anywhere, can't you?"

"Yes, but——" said Douglas uncertainly.

"Rivers are water, aren't they?" went on William, pursuing his theme, "an' ponds are water. The sea's just the same as a lot of rivers an' ponds stuck together, isn't it?"

"There's salt in the sea," said Henry triumphantly.

"Well, you can put salt in a pond, can't you?" snapped William. "Don't keep makin' such silly objections. Salt's cheap enough, isn't it?"

"There's sand at the sea-side," said Ginger.

"Well, what's sand but yellow earth?" said William. "I bet it's easy enough to turn earth yellow. Come to that, there's lots of sand where they're makin' those new houses. I bet I could bring down enough to make a sea-side. They stop workin' there at five."

"But—there's piers an' promenades an' pierrots at the sea-side," said Henry.

"Well, what's piers but a bit of wood stuck out into the water? An' a promenade's only a bit of ground for walkin' about on, an' pierrots only people with their faces blacked. All you want to make a sea-side is a bit of water an' a bit of salt an' a bit of wood an' a bit of ground an' some blacking. I bet I could make one's easy's easy. We'd charge money, of course, for lettin' people come to it. I bet we'd make a jolly lot of money."

The others were becoming interested in the project despite themselves.

"There's rock," said Henry.

"Well, rock's only humbug," said William. "An' jus' think. There's lots of water here. I bet we could make it a sea-side in no time if we set about it prop'ly."

"Which shall we start with," said Ginger, "pond or river?"

"River," said William. "There's more of it. I bet I can fix up a pier an' all the rest of it all right. We'll charge a penny to come in an' a penny for all the things. We'll have all the same things they have at the sea-side—donkey rides an' suchlike."

"Who'll give the donkey rides?" said Douglas.

"You," said William promptly.

"All right," said Douglas after a moment's silence in which he wondered whether to consider this an insult or an honour and decided, finally, that it would be less trouble to consider it an honour.

"There'll be a jolly lot to think about," said Ginger.

"Well, we can think about it, can't we?" said William. "I bet I'm as good at thinkin' about things as anyone. If everyone was as frightened of thinkin' about things as you, nothin'd ever get done, anywhere. What about hist'ry? How d'you think Charles Ist'd've got the Magna Charter an' suchlike signed if he hadn't thought about it?"

The others were silent, suspecting some historical inaccuracy, but not sure enough of their ground to correct it.

"An' Nelson an' Waterloo an' all those other gen'rals——" went on William.

"Waterloo wasn't a gen'ral," said Henry.

"Well, whatever he was," conceded William airily, "he'd never've given a thing up jus' 'cause it wanted a bit of thinkin' about."

"He wasn't a man at all. He was a battle," said Henry.

"Don't care what he was," said William. "I bet he'd've made a sea-side without all this fuss."

The idea of the local sea-side was gradually becoming attractive, and in the light of William's optimism the difficulties were melting away.

" '*Course* we'll make money," said William, waving aside their objections almost before he had heard them.

"We'll make a jolly lot of money. More than we've ever made before. Yes, I know," impatiently, "we've done things to make money before an' they didn't make it. But this is diff'rent. We've never had a sea-side before, have we? Well, that proves it, doesn't it? It's somethin' quite new. Everyone'll like it. Why, all the people what aren't goin' to the sea-side——the ordin'ry sea-side, I mean—they'll be jolly glad to pay to come to it. You see, it'll be cheaper than the ordin'ry sea-side, 'cause there won't be the train fare. I bet once we've done it everyone'll be copyin' us an' no one'll ever bother to go to the real sea-side any more. Well, come on, anyway, an' let's get it all fixed up."

They gathered round, eagerly discussing details.

* * *

The inland sea-side was opened to the public the next Saturday. The public, in the persons of the Outlaws' contemporaries, had been duly canvassed and exhorted not to miss the chance of a lifetime.

"You'll never see anythin' like it again," William had said. "People'll start copyin' it all over the world, but this is the first an' none of the others will be as good as this. It's the finest sea-side you'll ever have seen. It's a jolly sight better than any ordin'ry sea-side. It's only a penny to come in, too. Jus' think of that. Only a penny. The sea-side for only a penny. You'll find *everythin'* the same as at the ordin'ry sea-side—even the sea. There's piers an' pierrots an' bands an'—an' everythin'."

"Do we have to pay for them extra?" demanded a member of his audience.

"Well, I like that!" said William indignantly. "I like that! The penny's same as your railway fare. Does your railway fare let you into the piers an' such-like at the ordin'ry sea-side? But everythin' at this sea-side's jolly cheap. Nothin's over a penny. Jus' think of that. Nothin's over a penny.''

He looked round hopefully, but the faces of his audience remained dour and suspicious.

"A penny?" said one of them bitterly. "That's jolly well a penny too much for any of *your* shows. We've had 'em before. We'd pay a penny not to come, more like.''

But William knew that curiosity would win the day, and that, even if they refused to pay their pennies for the various attractions, they would certainly pay their entrance money.

"It's different from anythin' we've ever done before," he said. "It'll be the best show anyone round here's ever been to. You come along on Sat'day an' see.''

They came along on Saturday. William and the Outlaws had taken a strip of the river-bank for their inland sea-side, posting notices on all the neighbouring bushes: "To the Seeside", with an arrow that, unfortunately, pointed the wrong way. Douglas had thrown a handful of salt into the water, more from the artist's desire for correctness in every detail than because he really thought that it would transform the river to salt water. Henry had carried several buckets of sand from the new houses and scattered it lightly over the soil at the edge of the river. There happened to be stepping-stones across the river at this point, and William had balanced a plank of wood along the first three, labelling it "Peer 1d." The path by the side of the river had a large notice, "Prommynard 1d." and an old tub, with two clothes props leaning against it, was designated "Spead Boat 1d." William and his friends had often taken their places in this (it held one with comfort and two with discomfort) and propelled it for a few yards in shallow water before it overturned. Two soap-boxes were set up by the path. On one was arrayed a number of humbugs beneath a notice "Seeside Rock 1d. each," and on the other were some biscuits and old sardine and fruit tins, filled with water, labelled "Teas 1d." William and Douglas were in charge of these attractions. Henry, equipped with two tin trays and a trumpet, was the band. Ginger, his face (and collar) caked with blacking, was the pierrot. As the patrons scrambled down the bank from the road to the riverside, William took up his position at the bottom to collect their entrance money in a cardboard boot-box.

A fair proportion of the juvenile population of the neighbourhood seemed to have come, but they had not come in the spirit of grateful enthusiasm for which William had hoped. They were critical, reserved, disapproving. They were led, William saw to his dismay, by a long-nosed, red-headed girl who rejoiced in the name of Arabella Simpkin, and who was expert in discovering the weak spots of anyone and anything, and in pointing them out to others. She was, moreover, a girl of dominant personality and had more than once wrecked William's schemes.

"Oh," he said bitterly, "so you've come, have you?"

"Yes," she retorted with spirit. "An' why shouldn't I, I'd like to know? My penny's as good as anyone else's, isn't it? Or isn't it?" she added pugnaciously.

"Yes, yes," said William pacifically. "Yes, of course it is."

"Yes, an' I've gotter find out first whether this show's worth a penny," she went on grimly. "If it isn't——" She gave him a sinister look and left the sentence unfinished.

"I bet you'll find it is," William assured her. "There's a pier an' a promenade."

"Where?" said Arabella, looking round.

"There," said William, pointing to them. "Only a penny each."

"Penny *each*!" said Arabella indignantly. "D'you think I'm goin' to pay a penny for *those*? I can jolly well walk on an ole plank anywhere for nothin' an' I'm goin' to here, too."

She proceeded to walk along the "pier", her nose aquiver with contempt. "Pier!" she ejaculated scornfully. "Pier indeed!"

The other patrons were inspecting the rest of the attractions. Two of them had entered the "speed boat" and were now emerging, dripping and howling, from the water. Several more had attacked the "sand" and were expressing intense indignation at finding the substratum of muddy soil immediately beneath. William reasoned patiently with the malcontents.

"Well, you didn't push it off right. You did it too hard. You oughter've done it more gradual. Well, I can't help you being wet. It's only the same as any other speed boat. You've gotter know how to manage it. Any speed boat'd upset if you didn't treat it right. An' I don't know why you're grumbling at me when you've gone and ruined our speed boat. Look at it now—upside down an' right out in the middle where no one can get at it. Oh, all right, *go* home. I don't want to stop you, an'— all right, *have* your penny back, if you don't think it's worth it. It's worth a jolly sight more'n a penny, let me tell you. There's nothin' wrong with this sea-side. It's you what don't know how to *act* at a sea-side. You don't deserve to go to one. All right, I'm sorry you came, too, an' I'm jolly glad you're goin'. Well, what's wrong with

"SO YOU'VE COME, HAVE YOU?" SAID WILLIAM BITTERLY.

the sand? I know it's not sand underneath, but it's the same as sand. Sand's only yellow earth, isn't it? That's all sand is. Well, this is jus' the same as sand 'cept that it's not yellow underneath. You can dig in it—can't you?—same as sand, an' make castles an' pies an'

"AN' WHY SHOULDN'T I?" RETORTED ARABELLA. "MY PENNY'S AS
GOOD AS ANYONE ELSE'S."

suchlike. Well, dig harder, then, if it's too hard. I
thought it would be more fun havin' it a bit harder.
Ordin'ry sand's too soft. Oh, all right, then, *go* home. I
don't want you to stay."

Arabella had now approached the rock stall, where the humbugs were displayed beneath the notice: "Rock 1d. each."

"What!" she ejaculated in disgust. "Penny each for those! Penny *each*?"

"They're sea-side rock," explained William.

"Sea-side rock!" exploded Arabella. "Sea-side *rock* indeed! They're jus' ordin'ry humbugs, same as you get at the post office."

The others, who, sheeplike, took their tone from Arabella, agreed.

"*Sauce!*" exploded Arabella.

"*Sauce!*" exploded the others.

They passed on to the "Teas."

"What's this?" said Arabella.

"Teas," explained William. "You c'n have a glass of water an' a biscuit for a penny."

"Call *that* a tea!" said Arabella. "Where's the glasses, anyway?"

"They're tins. They're jus' same as glasses. They're clean."

"Clean!" echoed Arabella passionately. "Clean! Call that clean?" She shivered with exaggerated horror. "I'd sooner die of thirst than drink out of one of those ole tins." She appealed to her followers: "Wouldn't you?"

Vociferously they agreed that they would.

"An' one ole biscuit for a penny!" went on Arabella. "Water's free an' ole tins are free. That means one ole biscuit for a penny. *Sauce!*"

"*Sauce!*" echoed her followers again.

They passed on to the band. Henry beat his trays and blew his trumpet frenziedly.

"What's that?" said Arabella coldly.

"It's the band," explained William.

"The what?" said Arabella.

"The band," repeated William, a note of pleading in his voice. "It's a jolly good band. If you shut your eyes you'd think it was a real one."

"If I shut my eyes I'd think it was a lunatic asylum, more like," said Arabella grimly. "An' what's this?"

They had now reached the blackened Ginger, who at once began to caper about in a somewhat ungainly "dance".

"He's the pierrot," explained William. "He's dancin'."

"Call that dancing?" said Arabella.

"Go on. Do somethin' else," William urged his exhibit. "Sing or somethin'."

"Give me time to get my breath," said Ginger irritably. " 'Sides, you don't tell 'em what to do next. You've jus' got to wait an' see what they do next, same as real ones."

"Well, I'm sick of watchin' him floppin' about," said Arabella.

"I'm not floppin' about," snapped Ginger. "I'm dancin'. All right, I'll sing. Jus' gimme time to think of somethin'."

"You don't know anythin'," jibed Arabella.

"I jolly well do," said Ginger indignantly. "I know a jolly lot. I know—well, tell me somethin' an' I bet I'll sing it all right."

"Nancy Lee," said Arabella.

"I wouldn't sing a soppy song about a girl even if I knew it," said Ginger, with increasing indignation. "I'd sing you one called 'Drinking, drinking, drinking', only I've forgotten how it starts. It goes low down like this"—he drew in his chin and emitted a deep hoarse croak.

"Oh, shut up," said Arabella. "That's not singing. Can't you do anythin' else?"

"He can do acrobatics," said William. "Go on, Ginger, do acrobatics."

Ginger obediently turned two cart-wheels, then balanced for a precarious second on his hands before he overbalanced.

"Is that all?" said Arabella.

"No, he can do lots more things," said William, while Ginger looked at him apprehensively, wondering what next would be demanded of him.

But Arabella had had enough.

"It's a rotten show," she pronounced, "an' if you think we're goin' to pay a penny for it you're jolly well thinkin' wrong an'——" She turned to her followers. "Isn't it a rotten show?" she demanded.

They agreed vociferously

"Come on," shouted Arabella. "Let's smash everything up an' get back our pennies."

The Outlaws glanced around them. They were hopelessly outnumbered. Nothing seemed to remain but ignominious disaster—a disaster that would be remembered against them for years.

"Listen," pleaded William desperately, while Douglas, who was in charge of the boot-box, made ineffectual efforts to conceal himself behind a bush. "Listen. There's somethin' else we've not shown you yet."

The malcontents stopped for a moment and looked at him expectantly.

"I'll tell you if you'll jus' listen," said William, racking his brains to think of something. "Jus' listen. I'll tell you in a minute if you'll jus' listen."

They had turned to him expectantly, but their expectancy was now changing to anger. Arabella seized the luckless Douglas and dragged him from behind his bush, while willing hands prepared to rifle the boot-box.

"*Listen*, won't you?" implored William urgently, "an' I'll tell you what this other thing is . . ."

There was a short silence, in which William's mind remained still hopelessly empty of ideas. He was on the point of owning himself beaten when—something dropped from the tree above on to his shoulder. He turned and stared at it in incredulous amazement. It couldn't be . . . it was . . . it couldn't be . . . it was. It was a small perky-looking monkey in a red coat and a little porter's cap. There was a collar round its neck on which William could read the word "Jacko".

Almost immediately it jumped down from his shoulder to the ground, picked up a twig, shouldered it, and began to march up and down in military fashion. The children crowded round with cries of excitement. William quickly rallied his forces. He didn't know where the monkey had come from or whose it was, but it had arrived in the nick of time.

"*There!*" he said triumphantly. "Din' I say there was somethin' else? I din' want to tell you jus' what it was till the time came."

"William, it's lovely," said Arabella in a voice that quivered with ecstasy and a strange new humility. "William, I'm sorry I said all those things. I didn't mean any of them. May I touch it?"

"No," said William firmly. "It's a jolly expensive monkey. I can't have people messin' it about." He glanced round at the circle of intent faces and decided to strike while the iron was hot.

"It's extra," he informed them. 'It's twopence each to watch it."

"WILLIAM," SAID ARABELLA, "IT'S LOVELY."

There were hasty confabulations, and coppers were exchanged, as the indigent borrowed from the wealthy, and small grubby hands, containing the requisite two pennies, were eagerly extended to William.

"It's lovely, William," they said in propitiatory voices. "It's a lovely show. We didn't mean any of the

"DIDN'T I SAY THERE WAS SOMETHING ELSE IN THE SHOW?" SAID
WILLIAM TRIUMPHANTLY.

things we said. We didn't know about the monkey then,
you see. William, may we just touch it?"

"It's a halfpenny extra to touch it," said William.

Halfpennies were eagerly proffered, and small grubby

hands, trembling with excitement, were stretched out to
the monkey. The monkey, apparently, had no objec-
tion. It laid down its musket and shook hands graciously,
taking hold of a finger and shaking it up and down. It
touched its cap. Finally, to the delight of the audience, it
began to turn cart-wheels in the grass. There seemed, in
fact, to be no end to its tricks. It evidently considered
William its owner, and, when tired of performing,
sprang on to his shoulder and nestled against him affectionately, stroking his hair and patting his cheek. William was in the seventh heaven of rapture. But the joy
had an undercurrent of anxiety. He kept picturing the
real owner searching desperately for his lost pet. William was not imaginative, but he could not help realising
something of the anguish that he must be feeling. To
own this paragon and then to lose him ! After all, he had
had him now for nearly half an hour, and the show had
been turned by him from a fiasco into a glorious success.
Perhaps he ought to go and reconnoitre and see if he
could find the owner. He transferred the monkey to
Ginger's shoulder, said, "You keep him a bit," and
made his way up the embankment to the road. Roars of
laughter followed him, for Jacko was now jabbering
away excitedly in a high-pitched voice and pointing at
various members of the crowd, with a little brown finger,
as he did so.

William scrambled up on to the road and looked about
him. The road was empty. On the other side of it was a
stretch of common-land, with bushes and tall bracken.
Suddenly he saw a man coming from behind one of the
bushes. He carried a barrel-organ and was searching
about in the undergrowth. He saw William and came up
to him scowling. He had an ugly, ill-tempered face,
adorned by several days' growth of beard. William

couldn't bear the thought of handing over his beloved Jacko to his care.

" 'Ere!" said the man. "You seen a monkey anywhere on this road?"

"No," said William, assuring himself that he only spoke the literal truth. He hadn't seen a monkey on that road. The man was growling angrily to himself. Suddenly he put the barrel-organ behind a bush.

"Keep an eye on that," he said to William, "while I have a look round for him. He's hiding somewhere about here. I had him a minute ago, blast him!"

He went off over the common, moving the bracken and looking behind the bushes, cursing softly to himself. William stood by the barrel-organ, inspecting it with interest. You just turned the little handle and the tune came. He wanted to try it . . . but if he did, of course, the cross man would come back, crosser than ever. He looked longingly over the road. Hilarious sounds still came from the now successful sea-side show. If he could just slip down with it for a moment! He'd bring it back before the cross man had finished looking for the monkey. A barrel-organ *and* a monkey! If he could have them together life would be perfect and complete. He seized the barrel-organ, dragged it out from the bush, and staggered with it across the road and down the embankment to the riverside. Glancing round, he saw that the cross man was still continuing his search among the undergrowth. The sea-side patrons greeted his appearance with shouts of applause. Jacko jabbered still more excitedly and leapt upon the organ, where he held out his cap and saluted the gathering. William, realising that the sound of the instrument would attract the attention of the cross man, contented himself with turning an imaginary handle on the other side from the real one. It was almost as good as the real one, and the children formed a ring and danced round him, shouting with joy. Suddenly he heard voices from the road—one excited, almost tearful, the other calm and majestic. He heard the words "monkey" and "organ". Handing Jacko and the barrel-organ into Ginger's charge again, he crept up the embankment to investigate. A small dark man, with a little wistful face rather like the monkey's, was talking animatedly to a somewhat bewildered policeman.

"An' when I woke up zey had gone," he was saying, "my Jacko and my beautiful organ. Gone. Both gone. I make enquiries. I find which way ze thief went. I follow him. I make enquiries all along ze road. I follow quickly. I love my little Jacko as if he was my child. No one but me can look after him. I trace ze thief to zis village, but now I am too exhausted to go on furzer and zen I see ze policeman and think: 'I will tell him my troubles. He will help.' "

The policeman slowly took out his note-book.

"Yes," he said. "But why didn't you go to the police station at once?"

The little man spread out his hands.

"Ze police station? I know not where it is."

"There was a chap nosin' about the bushes when I came along," said the policeman. "Went off down the road like a streak o' lightning when he saw me. I wondered what he'd been up to. Suppose it couldn't have been him, could it?"

The little dark man shook his head.

"Not if he had not ze monk an' ze organ. Ze organ I should not mind so much. It is ze thought of my Jacko that distresses me. He is like my child to me—so affectionate, so charming. Ze thought of anyone being unkind to him—it lacerates me. It——"

"Yes, yes, yes," said the policeman. "Now tell me just what happened. When did you first miss your organ? 'Ere!" He looked down at William, who had suddenly appeared between them. "What are you hangin' about for? Off you go!"

"I've got 'em," said William

"Got what?" said the policeman.

"His monkey and his organ," said William.

"Now, none of your sauce," said the policeman. "Do as you're told and clear off."

Suddenly the loud strains of "I want to be happy" rent the air. Ginger, left in charge, had not been able to resist the temptation to turn the handle. The policeman and the little dark man stared at each other. It was unmistakably a barrel-organ. It came unmistakably from the direction of the embankment. Together they plunged down the grassy bank. A scene of wild festivity met their eyes. Ginger stood turning the handle of the barrel-organ. Jacko sat on it, waving his cap hilariously in a brown skinny paw. A ring of children danced around, shouting, singing, laughing.

"My Jacko! My organ!" said the little dark man, almost weeping with joy.

He seized William's hands and began to dance around with him.

The policeman stood looking on at the scene in amazement, conquering a strong desire to join in the dance.

Having conquered it, he took out his note-book and said:

" 'Ere, 'ere, 'ere! Stop all this row."

But nobody listened to him.

Chapter 2

William and the Little Strangers

THE Outlaws sat round the old barn engaged in desultory conversation. They were all feeling slightly bored.

"Farmer Jenks gotter new cart," said Ginger. "It only came yesterday."

"I know," said William. "I saw it. There's nothin' excitin' about that. It's jus' the same as the ole one, only new."

"Well, then, it can't be jus' the same as the ole one," said Ginger aggressively.

"Oh, shut up," said William, who was feeling too bored to argue.

"Victor Jameson's got measles," said Douglas.

"Well, that's no good to me," said William irritably. "I never catch anythin'. I'm tired of tryin'. I was playin' with George Bell when he was all over scarlet fever spots, but I never got it. I never have any luck. I've never had anythin' as long as I can remember," he went on pathetically. "I hardly know what grapes taste like."

"His grandmother's sent him a big basket of fruit, an' his aunt's given him a new train with a station."

"Oh, shut up," said William.

There was another long silence.

"What's pygmies?" said Douglas at last.

"A kid's name for pigs," said William.

"No, it isn't," said Douglas, "that's piggies."

"I know," said Henry. "They're grown-ups but same size as children."

"Gosh!" said William, suddenly interested. "They mus' look queer. But I bet there aren't any, *really*," he went on despondently. "There never is anythin' interestin', really. They're jus' fairy-tale stuff."

"No, they're not," said Douglas, " 'cause my aunt went to a lecture on 'em. All about a man what'd found 'em. He'd found 'em livin' in the middle of a wood an' they'd been there for years an' years an' years an' no one'd found 'em till the man did."

"When was it?" said William. "In hist'ry? I don't b'lieve any of the things that happened in hist'ry. I b'lieve they're all made up jus' to give us a lot of trouble learnin' 'em."

"No, it wasn't in hist'ry," Douglas assured him. "It was now. This man what found 'em's only jus' got back. He's got photos an' things of 'em."

"Did he *leave* 'em there?" said William incredulously.

"Yes. They were sort of savages, you see. They'd been there for years an' years an' years, an' no one'd found 'em till this man found 'em."

"I jolly well wouldn't've *left* 'em there," said William. "I'd've brought 'em all home with me. I'd like to have a lot of savages of my own. Where did he find 'em?"

"Some foreign place," said Douglas vaguely.

"If it'd been in England, I'd have gone after 'em myself," said William. Then he sat up, as though galvanised by a sudden idea. "I say!" he said. "I bet

there *are* some in England. They'd been in this place for
years an' years without anyone findin' 'em. Well, why
shun't they've been in England for years an' years,
too?"

"Well . . . it's sort of diff'rent in England," said
Douglas uncertainly.

"No, it isn't," said William. "There's woods in England, isn't there? Well, that's where they hide, isn't it?"

"Yes, but . . . someone'd've found 'em in England
before now."

"I bet they wouldn't," said William. "I bet no one's
ever gone over every inch of every wood. There's
hundreds an' hundreds an' *hundreds* of miles of woods
in England. An', even if anyone did, I bet these pygmy
people could hide from 'em all right. They could creep
about under bushes an' suchlike. I bet I could if I was
one, anyway."

"Well, then, *you* couldn't find 'em," said Ginger,
who saw where William's thoughts were tending.

"I bet I could," said William. "You can find people
your own size while you can't find 'em if they're smaller.
I bet there *are* some in England, an' I bet I'm goin' to
find 'em. I'm goin' to jolly well have a try, anyway."

"It might be dangerous," said Douglas. "They might
be savage."

"I bet I can be savage, too, if they are."

"When are you goin' to start?" said Henry.

"Now," said William, rising. "I'm jus' about sick of
nothin' happenin'. Come on. Let's go an' look for
pygmies."

*   *   *

They decided to start with the woods round Marleigh,
which were less familiar to them than those round their

own village. William headed the band, then came Ginger, then Douglas, then Henry.

"We'd better not make too much noise," said William, "or we'll be scarin' 'em away. I bet they can get away jolly easy under bushes an' things."

"Do they talk English?" demanded Ginger.

" 'Course not," said Douglas. "They talk pygmy langwidge."

"We'll teach 'em English," said William. "They'll be jolly grateful to us. It's a jolly sight easier to talk than any foreign langwidge. I can never think why everyone in the world doesn't talk it—an easy langwidge like English—'stead of worryin' over verbs an' stuff like what you have to in foreign langwidges an' pronouncin' the words all wrong."

"P'r'aps it's easy to them," suggested Henry tentatively.

" '*Course* it isn't," said William. "It couldn't be easy to *anyone*. Why, look at me. I can talk English 's easy 's easy without even havin' to learn it, but it takes me hours an' hours to do a French exercise, an' even then I get it all wrong. Well, that *proves* it doesn't it? I can't think why anyone ever started foreign langwidges. There isn't any sense in them."

They agreed, but without much enthusiasm. They had heard William on this subject so often that they had lost interest in it.

"Listen," he said suddenly.

There was a faint rustling in the undergrowth.

"I bet that's a pygmy," said William, plunging in to investigate.

" 'Spect it was a rabbit," said Ginger, when a thorough search had revealed nothing.

"No, it was a pygmy all right," said William, "but

they get away so quick. That's why no one's found 'em all these years. We'll be jolly quiet an' then I 'spect we'll come on 'em sudden. Let's not talk for a bit.''

For two and a half minutes they walked in silence. Then William said:

"We ought to've brought somethin' to give 'em to tame 'em. Sweets or somethin' like that. I say, let's get some sweets now. I've gotter penny. How much've the rest of you got?"

Together they produced fourpence halfpenny, and Douglas was despatched to Marleigh to spend it at the village shop. He returned with a bag of liquorice all-sorts.

"They're the cheapest," he said, handing it to William, "an' she put two more on after it went down, so it ought to be all right."

"It depends how many there are of them, of course," said William, inspecting it anxiously. "If there's hundreds of 'em we'd better jus' give these to the high-up ones to tame 'em and let 'em tame the others."

"Let's jus' have one each to make sure they're all right," suggested Ginger.

"No," said William firmly, putting the packet into his pocket. "Once we start on 'em there won't be any left. There never is. No, we'll keep 'em all to tame these pyg people."

"We'll eat 'em if we don't find any, won't we?" said Ginger, who was beginning to feel hungry and thought that a liquorice allsort in the hand was worth any amount of pygmies in the bush.

"Oh, yes, of course," agreed William.

"How long'll we give ourselves?"

"We'll finish these woods first," said William. "I bet, even if we don't find 'em, they're here all right. They're jolly good at hidin', you know. I 'spect they spend all their spare time practisin' it."

They were growing a little tired and their interest in the pygmy race was waning.

"Shun't be surprised if it's not all a mess-up with fairies," said Ginger. "You know. Someone got 'em mixed."

"*Fairies!*" exploded William contemptuously.

"No, it isn't," persisted Douglas. "I *know* it isn't. This aunt of mine said this man had seen them, an' they were about the same size as children."

"I bet this aunt of yours was dreamin'," said William.

"No, she axshully went to this lecture," persisted Douglas. "I saw her go."

"Well, she went to sleep in it same as everyone does in lectures," said William, "an' dreamed all this pygmy stuff, an' when she woke up at the end she thought the lecture'd been about 'em. You tell her she's wasted a whole afternoon for us, an'——"

"I think I've read about them," said Henry doubtfully.

"No, you haven't," said William. "You're only swankin'. You're always pretendin' you've read about things that other people've never heard of. I think that Douglas's aunt went to sleep in this lecture same as I said an'——"

He stopped. They had come to a clearing in the wood, and there, sitting round in disconsolate attitudes, was a company of people the size of children, some with beards, some with moustaches, dressed in strange garments. They turned and gazed at the Outlaws indifferently.

"It's *them!*" gasped William.

The four Outlaws stood open-mouthed. Now that they had actually come upon their quarry they had not the least idea how to deal with it. Then William remembered the packet of liquorice allsorts and, taking it out of his pocket, handed it round. The pygmies accepted the gift, munched with obvious appreciation, and waited for more.

"That's tamed 'em," said William triumphantly. "I knew it would."

WITH SWEEPING GESTURES, WILLIAM INTIMATED TO HIS CAPTIVES
THAT THEY WERE TO ACCOMPANY HIM.

"Now, perhaps, you'll believe my aunt," said Douglas.

The pygmies were talking to each other in a strange language. The Outlaws listened with interest.

"Pygmy language," explained Henry, with an air of deep wisdom.

"Well, what are we goin' to do with 'em now we've got 'em?" demanded Ginger.

THE QUEER LITTLE STRANGERS WERE QUITE WILLING TO OBEY HIM.

"We'll take 'em back with us," said William, "an' keep 'em in the old barn."

"How can you tell 'em you've captured 'em? You can't speak pygmy."

"No, but I can show 'em. They're tame, now. There's a few more liquorice allsorts left, too, if they start getting savage."

Beckoning with his fingers, making sweeping gestures with his arms, William intimated to his captives that they were to accompany him. They acquiesced with unexpected docility, still talking among themselves, and followed the Outlaws to the old barn. There they sat down in obedience to a gesture from William, and the liquorice allsorts were handed round again. The captives seemed quite placid and unperturbed, as if they were accustomed to being captured.

"Well," said Ginger again, "what're we goin' to do with 'em now we've got 'em?"

William was feeling slightly nonplussed. Somehow he'd never looked beyond the actual capture of the pygmies.

"I could lecture on 'em same as this man what found 'em did," he suggested rather doubtfully.

"My aunt's been to one lecture," said Ginger. "She won't want to go to another."

"I jolly well don't want your aunt," said William with spirit. "There's plenty of other people in the world besides your aunt, isn't there?"

"No one what'd come to hear *you* lecture."

"Why not?" said William. "I bet I could lecture as well as any grown-ups."

Ginger decided to abandon that particular argument. "What are you goin' to do with 'em now, anyway?" he said. "They'll want food. If you don't give 'em food they'll die of hunger an' then you'll get hung for murder, an' we've not got enough money to buy 'em food. We've spent it all on the liquorice allsorts."

"Well, I'm not goin' to let 'em go," said William, "now I've had all the trouble catchin' 'em. Why, the world'll ring with our names, once people know about them."

He glanced at the pygmies. They were still talking animatedly among themselves in the unknown language.

"Let's teach 'em tricks an' hire 'em out to circuses an' things," suggested Ginger. "We'll make a lot of money that way."

"Yes, we might do that," admitted William. "I bet it'd be a bit difficult to teach 'em tricks, though. One of 'em's quite old. I bet he wouldn't learn anythin'." They glanced at the small figure with the long white beard who seemed to be the centre of the group. "I 'spect he's the king," he went on. "I wish we could talk pygmy. It's goin' to be a nuisance not bein' able to talk pygmy to 'em."

At this moment Violet Elizabeth Bott appeared suddenly in the doorway. She was a damsel of six years old, whose parents lived at the Hall and who took an (in the Outlaws' eyes) undue interest in all the Outlaws' doings.

"Go away," said William. "We don't want you."

Violet Elizabeth was accustomed to this mode of greeting. She would indeed have been disconcerted by any other.

"What are you doing?" she said, entering the barn with that supreme self-assurance that was her most marked characteristic.

"I told you we didn't want you," said William severely. "You've got ears, haven't you? Go away."

"If you don't want me here go away yourthelf," retorted Violet Elizabeth, to whom the letter "s" had always presented insuperable difficulties, and added serenely, "an' I'll go with you if you do. Anyway," she went on after a pause, "you've not bought the world, have you? People can be in the thame plathe ath other people, can't they? There'th no law againth it, ith there?" Violet Elizabeth had copied William's own methods of argument and William found them disarming. "Who are they, anyway?" she demanded, pointing to the pygmies.

"Pygmies," said William shortly. "Now you know, you can shut up and go away."

"Where've they come from?" she asked.

"We found 'em," said Ginger. "They've been livin' in Marleigh woods for hundreds an' hundreds of years without anyone findin' 'em, an' now we've found 'em, so they b'long to us. We've not made up our minds what we're goin' to do with 'em yet."

"Give me one," said Violet Elizabeth, adding coaxingly, "*pleath*."

"No, we won't," said William indignantly. "You've gotter nerve, too, asking. You come in here without being asked and then start tryin' to pinch our pygmies."

Violet Elizabeth pouted.

"Well, you've got"—she counted—"theven of them. I only want a little one." She pointed to the smallest of the group. "I'll have that one."

"No, you won't," said William. "You *can't*. They b'long to us."

"I only want the little one," pleaded Violet Elizabeth.

"No," said William.

"I'll take *thuch* care of it," said Violet Elizabeth.

"No."

"I'll thcream an' *thcream* if you won't let me have it."

William, unlike Violet Elizabeth's mother, was unmoved by the threat.

"All right," said William. "Thcream an' thcream, then. Go on. Thcream an' thcream. I don't care."

Violet Elizabeth obviously wondered whether to fulfil her threat and finally decided not to. It was no use wasting good tactics on someone who couldn't appreciate them. She considered the matter a moment in silence.

"Will you thell it to me?" she said at last.

William looked at her, interested.

"How much'll you give?" he asked.

"Thixpenth," said Violet Elizabeth promptly.

William was secretly impressed at the munificence of this offer. He had expected her to offer a penny and he'd meant to beat her up to twopence. He looked round at his captives. They were now watching him rather sullenly and muttering to each other in tones that were unmistakably hostile. They were getting wild again, thought William. It was high time they were soothed by some more liquorice allsorts. The sixpence would come in very handy.

"All right," he said at last, "but we're jolly well not sellin' more than one, an' you can't choose. You've gotter have the little one."

"Thath the one I want," said Violet Elizabeth happily.

She opened a small purse that hung from her shoulder by a strap, took out a miniature handkerchief, a shell, a limp daisy chain, a snapshot of herself, and, finally, with an air of triumph, a sixpence.

"Thanks," said William, taking it.

He looked uncertainly from Violet Elizabeth to her purchase.

"I can't tell him you've bought him," he said. "I can't speak pygmy. Jus' think," he went on bitterly, "of all

VIOLET ELIZABETH TOOK HIM BY THE HAND AND LED HIM ACROSS
THE FIELD.

the time they've wasted in school teachin' us a langwidge like French what no one ever needs, when they might've been teachin' us a useful langwidge like pygmy. If we'd learnt pygmy we could've explained it all to them."

Violet Elizabeth was smiling sweetly at the smallest of the strangers.

"Come on," she said persuasively. "I'll take thuch care of you. My nameth Violet Elithabeth. Whath yourth?"

The smallest pygmy glowered at her from under his eyebrows and said something (presumably not flattering) in the unintelligible tongue.

"You'll have to tame him," said William. "Liquorice allsorts tames 'em best, but I expect any sort of sweet'd do."

Violet Elizabeth burrowed again in the small leather purse and drew out two paper-wrapped sweets. She unwrapped one and held it out to the smallest pygmy. He took it, inspected it, put it in his mouth, then, after testing it frowningly, smiled with sudden friendliness. Violet Elizabeth showed him the other, and, taking him by the hand, led him gently from the barn and across the field. He accompanied her without resistance, holding her hand and looking up at her trustingly. As they vanished from sight, the Outlaws saw Violet Elizabeth take off her leather purse and hang it over the shoulder of her new possession, thus endowing him with all her worldly wealth.

William turned to the others.

"Let's teach 'em games," he said. "We'll pick up sides. I'll start. I'll have this one."

He touched the white-bearded pygmy, who, evidently taking the gesture as a sign of hostility, immediately flung himself upon him. The other pygmies followed his example, and in a second the barn was full of scuffling shouting combatants. The beards and moustaches came off early in the struggle. It was a fight of the "all against all" sort. Outlaws and pygmies pummelled themselves and each other indiscriminately.

*   *   *

Miss Marcia Gillespie, the headmistress of the Marleigh Rational School for Children, had spent a very enjoyable month touring the Baltic States. In Lithuania she had met a kindred soul, who happened also to be the headmistress of a school for young children. Miss Gillespie could not speak Lithuanian, and the Lithuanian headmistress could not speak English, but they discussed in French such subjects as the beauty of child nature and the danger of repressing any manifestation of it, and found that their ideas were practically identical, for both belonged definitely to the "clouds of glory" school. They discovered, too, that each of them kept several children (whose parents were abroad or otherwise occupied) at her school during the holidays, and then, almost simultaneously, they had an idea. They would exchange pupils for the next holidays. Six or seven small Lithuanian boys should come to Marleigh Rational School the next holidays, and the same number of Miss Gillespie's pupils should go to the Lithuanian school.

They were energetic women, and no idea, once seized by them, ever had a chance of escape. Parents had to be consulted, red tape had to be carefully manipulated, but all obstacles melted away before the determination of the two redoubtable ladies. A Lithuanian mistress was to accompany the Lithuanians, an English mistress the English boys. The arrangement once made, Miss Marcia

Gillespie thought and dreamed of little else. She bought a Lithuanian grammar and studied it conscientiously, but without much success, for an hour a day. She drew out a programme for the visit. There were to be readings from the great English poets (they'd soon pick up English, she thought optimistically), rambles over the English countryside, collections of wild English flowers—in fact, a general education in the glorious culture of our glorious country. And, most important of all, there was to be the children's pageant.

It happened that last term Miss Gillespie had got up a children's pageant. She was a great believer in children's pageants as an educational force, and her latest effort had depicted Richard the Second as a child quelling the mob. She had taken a lot of trouble over the clothes, and she was rather glad to have an opportunity of using them again. She decided to repeat the performance and let the little strangers take part in it. She was aware, of course, that they couldn't take a very prominent part in it, but she intended them to represent a small group of older citizens who would reason with the mob in dumb show and induce it to accept the young king's mediation. She fixed a day and invited the neighbourhood. It was to take place two days after the arrival of the children, giving her a day to explain the situation to them and rehearse them in their parts.

But, to her dismay, the children did not arrive at the time they were expected. The formalities had taken longer than had been foreseen and, in fact, they had arrived only on the actual day of the performance. Miss Marcia Gillespie was distracted. To make matters worse, the Lithuanian schoolmistress who accompanied them was not a good traveller and arrived in a state of collapse. Miss Marcia Gillespie had only time to hustle her off to bed, to thrust the bewildered foreigners into their clothes and make-up, and lead them to the small clearing in the wood at the back of her garden. From this they were to make their way by a winding path to a small gate which would bring them out on to a conspicuous part of the lawn where the spectators were assembled. The other actors were to appear from the house, but it was thought that this would be a more impressive entry for the little strangers.

Miss Marcia Gillespie, in her very limited Lithuanian, informed the children that there was no time to rehearse, but that, if they stayed there till someone came for them and then did exactly what they were told, all would be well. She gave them a brief and not very illuminating description of what a pageant was and left them feeling that they now knew why everyone said the English were mad. They waited in the clearing till some boys came to fetch them, led them to an outhouse, and adopted towards them a proprietary attitude that they began to resent. They had no doubt at all that this was part of the pageant referred to by their hostess, and it was certainly no madder than everything else had been ever since they had arrived in this country. They stood it till flesh and blood could stand it no longer and then— and not till then—did they assert themselves.

*　　*　　*

At the Marleigh Rational School for Children the spectators were assembled on the lawn, taking their seats on the somewhat ramshackle collection of forms, chairs and benches provided by Miss Marcia Gillespie. Most of them had seen the pageant before but had been lured to the spot a second time by curiosity to see the small Lithuanians who were now taking part in it. Miss

Marcia Gillespie, thin, vague, and harassed, flitted about as usual, asking questions and not waiting for answers, greeting the same people several times over, giving the actors last injunctions that only made confusion worse confounded, and, at intervals, flying upstairs to pour eau-de-cologne upon the brow of the Lithuanian schoolmistress, who only wanted to be left alone. At last the pageant began. It began half an hour late, but, as no function of Miss Marcia Gillespie's had ever been known to begin less than half an hour late no one worried about that.

The mob came on—a bored and listless mob, whose threatening gestures suggested feeble greetings to friends in the audience. The young king appeared. He tripped over his robe, which brought his crown down on to his nose, and Miss Gillespie darted forward to straighten him. Her brooch caught in the ermine of his robe (cotton-wool cleverly inked over at intervals) and a large piece of it came away attached to her bosom. The more ill-bred of the spectators tittered. The young king held out his hand in what was meant to be a gesture of conciliation, but which looked as if he were pointing derisively at the leader of the mob. Then Miss Gillespie remembered the Lithuanians. She'd completely forgotten about them till this moment, and it was at this moment that they should appear—a noble body of steady responsible citizens, who should appeal to the frenzied mob to listen to the young king. She signed to the king and mob to go on making their gestures for a few moments longer and hurried round to the clearing in the wood to fetch her guests. It was empty. She called out distractedly and hunted among the bushes. There was no sign of them. She ran back to the scene of the pageant.

"They're gone!" she gasped.

The king and mob stopped making their gestures and stared at her. The audience rose and pressed forward concernedly. It had happened at last. They'd been prophesying a nervous breakdown for Marcia Gillespie for years.

"They're gone!" she sobbed.

The crowd made way for the father of the leader of the mob, who was a doctor.

"Get her to bed at once," he said. "Is there any sal volatile in the house?"

"But they're *gone*," screamed Miss Marcia Gillespie. "They're gone."

"Yes, yes, yes," said the doctor soothingly. "Yes, yes, yes. They're gone. Now come indoors and lie down."

"They were in the clearing in the wood and they're gone."

"Yes, yes, yes," agreed the doctor, who rather fancied himself with acute neurasthenic cases. Humour them. Always humour them. Agree with everything they say, however ridiculous. Keep them calm at all costs.

"Yes, yes, yes," he repeated. "They were in the clearing in the wood and they're gone. Yes, I know all about it."

"You know all about it?" panted Miss Gillespie. "Then why don't you *do* something?"

"That's all right," said the doctor soothingly. "Now all you've got to do is to rest."

"With those precious children *stolen*?" said Miss Gillespie wildly. "Kidnapped? Perhaps foully done to death?"

Slowly it dawned upon the doctor that there might be

more in this than a small *crise de nerfs*.

"What precious children?" he asked.

"My Lithuanians," sobbed Miss Marcia Gillespie.

The story came out. The Lithuanians, who had been waiting in the wood for their cue, had vanished. The whole party accompanied Miss Marcia Gillespie to the clearing and made a thorough search. Excited conversation arose on every side. Everyone had a different theory. They'd suddenly got homesick and run back to Lithuania. Someone had kidnapped them as a publicity stunt. They were pawns in some deep international game and were being used to ignite a world-wide conflagration. They were spies and, having gained the information they had come for, had returned to Lithuania, probably in an aeroplane that had been concealed in the clearing. They were hiding among the trees for a joke and would soon bounce out on the assembled company. They would never be seen or heard of again.

"Come, come, come, come," said a retired colonel, who had rather resented the doctor's taking charge of the situation. After all, he, the colonel, had once quelled, or almost quelled, a riot in India, and was the obvious person to deal with any situation. "Come, come, come! Let's all keep our heads. Let's do nothing rashly. The first thing to do is to get in touch with the police, of course."

"They're probably in the plot," said a small excited-looking woman with red hair. "They've probably been bribed by some foreign government. Obviously, there's far more in this than meets the eye. Seven children don't vanish from the landscape without some vast organisation being at the back of it. I mean, they don't know the country or the language. If they'd just wandered on to the road someone would have brought them back. No, it's some deep plot, cunningly conceived and cunningly carried out. Wheels within wheels, you know. The best brains in Europe."

The others were impressed but not convinced.

"Perhaps we'd better call in Scotland Yard at once," said Miss Gillespie tearfully, "without wasting any more time."

"Scotland Yard!" said the red-haired lady scornfully. "*They're* no good. No, the best thing to do would be to get in touch with the Home Secretary. The Secret Service ought to be put on to it without any delay at all."

"How *can* we get in touch with the Home Secretary?" said Miss Gillespie. "None of us know him."

"I suppose he's in the telephone book," said the red-haired lady impatiently.

But someone had gone quietly down to the village for the village policeman, who now appeared, note-book in hand.

"Seven of them, did you say?" he said, anxiously inspecting the point of his pencil. It was some time since he'd used it and it seemed to have vanished in the meantime. "P'r'aps you'd kindly write their names down," he went on tactfully to Miss Gillespie, handing her the note-book. She produced from her handbag a brand new pencil with a long tapering point. The policeman absent-mindedly took it from her with the note-book.

"Now, stand away, everyone," he said imperiously, then looked carefully into all the bushes near the clearing. Then he took out his note-book again.

"Disappeared between three and three thirty," he wrote slowly in his best handwriting with Miss Gillespie's pencil. "No clues."

*　　　*　　　*

The fight between the Outlaws and the pygmies in the old barn had finally developed into a good-natured scuffle, and friendly relations had been established in the process.

"What'll we do with 'em now?" said William to Ginger as they all sat down again, dishevelled and panting, but quite amicable.

"Let's take 'em out an' show 'em round a bit," suggested Ginger.

"All right," said William.

The gang sallied forth, scuffling in friendly fashion, and went down to the pond. There they finished the six-pennorth of liquorice allsorts, fished with sticks and bits of string and bent pins (provided by the Outlaws), paddled, and had races with "ships" consisting of bent twigs. The Lithuanians' spirits rose. Perhaps their stay here was not going to be so dull, after all. The English were not all mad. Here were four comparatively sane ones. After another indiscriminate wrestling match they all lay back on the grass, exhausted and happy.

"What'll we do with 'em next?" asked William.

"We ought to start civilisin' 'em," said Ginger. "That's what people do with savages."

"How d'you start?" said William with interest.

"You start makin' 'em wear proper clothes 'stead of those savage ones they've got on. I've got an aunt what does that for the heathen. She makes clothes an' sends them out to savage countries an' they make 'em take off their savage clothes an' put on those what my aunt makes."

"We'll do that, then," said William carelessly. "Has your aunt got any left over?"

"They wouldn't do even if she had," said Ginger. "She makes special ones for hot countries. These'd jus' have to have ordin'ry ones same as we have. I say, let's gettem them, shall we? Let's all go home an' fetch some clothes for 'em. I bet we can find enough."

They informed their new friends of their intention by signs. They were finding it extraordinarily easy to make themselves understood by signs. The pygmies signified assent and pleasure. They had been thrust reluctantly into these strange and excessively uncomfortable garments and were much relieved at the prospects of returning to more normal attire. The Outlaws ran to their homes to burrow among their possessions and—very furtively—crept back with their spoils. Each brought his Sunday suit, Ginger an overcoat as well, William a pair of running shorts. Thus they were all accommodated—for one of them wore the overcoat over his underclothes—and, leaving their pageant costumes on the bank, ran off with the Outlaws into the woods. William stopped to pick up one of the costumes and take it with him. He thought it would be useful if ever he wanted to play at being a pygmy.

*   *   *

It was the policeman who found the clothes by the river-bank. He carefully collected them, made a note to that effect in his note-book with Miss Marcia Gillespie's pencil, and brought them to her to be identified.

"The worst has happened," wailed Miss Marcia Gillespie when she heard his news, "the very worst . . . Oh, the villain, the villain—whoever did it!"

The Lithuanian mistress had been roused from sleep and the situation explained to her, but, as everyone was talking at the same time and as her knowledge of English was somewhat desultory, she thought that it was all part of the pageant and went to sleep again.

"We must have the pond dragged at once," said the red-haired woman.

"There are two survivors," said Miss Marcia Gillespie, who was counting the clothes. "Two of them must have escaped from the villain."

"This will mean a European war," said the red-haired woman darkly.

The policeman went off to make arrangements for dragging the pond.

Several of the people went to hunt for the survivors, but others took their places, as more friends and supporters and quite unknown passers-by came in to see what it was all about. Someone hoisted the Union Jack in a vague attempt to keep up the morale of the company, and someone else suggested singing the Lithuanian National Anthem, but, as no one knew it, the plan fell through.

The young Richard II, much relieved to be released from his role, made his way unobtrusively to the orchard, where he knew that Miss Gillespie had some trees of excellent dessert apples.

Then the news spread through the crowd.

A survivor had been found.

*   *   *

The Outlaws and the Lithuanians were playing Hide-and-seek in the woods, and William, by a piece of bad luck (or rather because wherever he was he couldn't help whistling), was found first and returned "home" to await the others. As time hung heavy on his hands he thought that he would try on the pygmy costume just to see what it felt like. It was on the small side but otherwise completely satisfactory. He decided that he felt exactly like a pygmy in it. He practised uttering the

unintelligible sounds that he thought of as the pygmy
language and then set off to the clearing in the wood,
where the pygmies had lived, to play at being one. He
wouldn't stay long. He'd be back before they'd all been
found. To reach that part of the wood he had to cross the
road. He was crossing it quite happily and unconcernedly
when a tall excited-looking man suddenly grasped him by
the shoulder. It was the colonel, who, having been ousted
from his position as controller of the situation by the red-
haired woman, had come out to look for clues, and, if
possible, steal a march on her that way.

"Who are you? Where are you going?" he said.

William was annoyed. He was playing at being a
pygmy and didn't want to be interrupted. He made the
unintelligible sounds of his own private pygmy language
in reply and made as if to go on his way, but the colonel,
wasting no more time, began to pull him along with him.
William struggled, then resigned himself, for the colonel
was powerfully built. But, although he resigned himself,
he decided still to be a pygmy. He wasn't going to have
his game spoilt by anyone. He was a pygmy and a pygmy
he'd remain. . . .

The crowd at Miss Marcia Gillespie's had increased
still further. A neighbouring tea-party, one member of
which was William's mother, Mrs. Brown, had, on
hearing the news, come in its entirety to see what could
be done and to offer condolences. The story of the
survivor increased excitement to fever pitch. The
colonel had telephoned to say that he'd found him
wandering helpless on the main road and was bringing
him up to Miss Gillespie's at once.

"I can't understand what he says," he said, "though,
of course, I recognise it to be Lithuanian. The boy seems
well physically but mentally dazed."

THE COLONEL SUDDENLY GRASPED WILLIAM BY THE SHOULDER.
"WHO ARE YOU?" HE DEMANDED. "WHERE ARE YOU GOING?"

The Lithuanian schoolmistress had at last gathered that her precious charges had vanished (the sinister discovery by the pond was at present being kept from her) and was displaying suitable emotion. The news of the survivor was being eagerly discussed on all sides.

"We can do nothing at all till we hear his story," said the red-haired woman. (She was annoyed that the colonel, and not she, had made the discovery. How that man did push himself in everywhere!) "His story should solve the whole mystery. We should then know the worst." She patted the sobbing Lithuanian schoolmistress on the back and murmured consolation in Italian, which was the only foreign language she knew and which she thought was better than nothing.

It was decided that the mob on the lawn might prove too overpowering for the little survivor and that the Lithuanian schoolmistress should receive him in the drawing-room in the presence of the policeman, specially recalled for the purpose, Miss Gillespie, and a few favoured friends.

"Such a pity," said the red-haired woman, "that the Chief of the Yard and the Home Secretary couldn't be here in time."

The colonel entered by the side door, dragging his unwilling captive with him and strode into the drawing-room. The Lithuanian schoolmistress flung herself sobbing on the small figure and pressed it to her bosom.

"Hadn't you better question the child?" said the colonel in Hindustani, which, not knowing Lithuanian, he thought would probably be near enough.

She held the child at arms' length then uttered a piercing scream. The policeman dropped his note-book.

"Coo, it's *'im*," he said, for William and he, as

breaker and guardian of the law respectively, were by no means strangers to each other.

The mob outside, roused by the scream, surged forward to the window. Mrs. Brown was caught on the crest of the wave and borne forward with the others. She gazed in at the window then uttered a scream as eloquent of horror as the Lithuanian schoolmistress's.

But whereas that lady had screamed because she didn't know the small boy in fourteenth-century costume who stood there scowling ferociously at her, Williams's mother screamed because she did.

It took, of course, a long time to settle things up. The youngest Lithuanian was the last to be restored. He was asleep in Violet Elizabeth's bed, sated with her sweets, and surrounded by the toys she had bestowed on him.

He liked Violet Elizabeth and had to be forcibly detached from her. Violet Elizabeth, on her side, persisted that she had paid for him and that no one had the right to take him away from her. Both wept loudly at the parting, and the youngest Lithuanian, during the rest of his stay in England, escaped so frequently from Miss Marcia Gillespie to the Hall, that in the end he was left there, for Violet Elizabeth's parents shared her partiality for him, and he returned finally to Lithuania, laden with presents and invitations to return.

With regard to the experiment as a whole Miss Marcia Gillespie had reluctantly to admit that it was not a success. The shocking trick played on her by that Brown boy was, of course, a bad beginning, and after that things just went from bad to worse. All the plans she had made for instilling the beautiful culture of our beautiful country into the little strangers came to nothing. They were out all day and every day, rampaging over the countryside with that dreadful Brown boy and his friends, and there was simply no doing anything with them.

The little Lithuanians, contrary to their expectations, thoroughly enjoyed their visit, but William will probably now to the end of his days continue to confuse the pygmy with the Lithuanian race.

Chapter 3

William to the Rescue

WILLIAM had always been interested in the spy question. He had, on several occasions, been convinced that he had found one of these nefarious plotters at work, had shadowed them and finally, as he thought, caught them red-handed, only to discover in each case that they were law-abiding citizens and that, instead of bringing a just punishment upon them, he had brought it on himself. His last attempt, indeed, had been so disastrous that he had sadly decided to leave the whole question alone in future. He had decided, too, even more sadly, that there were no spies in real life. If there had been, he'd have found one by now . . . But recent events had roused his interest in the subject afresh.

"Coo!" he said to the Outlaws after hearing his family discuss the news of the day. "Jus' fancy! Secret British papers comin' out in Italian newspapers an' suchlike. I bet there *are* a jolly lot of spies about, after all. I always said there was, but people wouldn't b'lieve me."

A sensational spy trial roused his interest still further. "Coo!" he said again. "Jus' fancy *that*! A German comin' over an' livin' ordin'ry in a cottage same as anyone else, an' all the time drawin' aeroplanes an' suchlike. There mus' be hundreds more what don't get caught. I bet really about every other person's a spy if only we knew it."

He aired these sentiments during tea at such length that his mother said mildly:

"Do stop talking so much, dear, and get on with your tea!"

"Yes, but jus' think of it," persisted William. "Jus' *think* of it! People all over the place stealin' papers an' drawin' aeroplanes an' half of them not even gettin' caught."

"Oh, *shut* up!" snapped Robert.

William looked at him curiously. Funny that Robert should get so mad at him for talking about spies. Of course, he was his own brother, but then every spy was somebody's brother. Funny him snapping at him like that if he hadn't got a guilty conscience. He decided to watch Robert very carefully. After all, spies were ordinary people with ordinary families that didn't know anything about them being spies. Yes, he'd begin his investigations with Robert. Robert, at first, seemed to promise very well. He was certainly odd in his behaviour. He would hurry out of the house directly after breakfast with a tense look on his face and not reappear till lunch. He would stay in his bedroom for long periods then sally forth, shining with cleanliness and hair oil, and dash off at once to some unknown destination, snapping "mind your own business" at William when he asked where he was going.

If there had been an aerodrome anywhere in the neighbourhood William would have had no doubts at all. But still—there was a Church Lads' Brigade Camp over at Marleigh, and, of course, even a spy had to start at the beginning and work up. Perhaps Robert was practising on the Church Lads' Brigade Camp, and when he'd stolen all their plans would go on to aerodromes and the War Office and that sort of thing. His suspicions were increased by hearing his mother say to his father that Robert had been very "mysterious" lately. He decided to shadow Robert for a day and see where he spent his time. It was no use charging him with his guilt, of course, till he had proofs.

He spent an uncomfortable afternoon shadowing Robert. Crawling along the ditch, he followed him to the village and then to a small, picturesque house just outside it that had been let for the summer months to a family consisting of a father, mother, and two daughters. Robert knocked and was admitted. William waited for a few minutes then crept up to the house and looked cautiously through the window. Robert was sitting in the front room with the elder of the two daughters—a pretty girl of about seventeen. He looked flushed and sheepish and painfully embarrassed, but was obviously trying to make a good impression, smiling languishingly, smoothing back his hair and straightening his tie, while he evidently racked his brains for something to say. Robert was susceptible but not a good conversationalist.

William watched with scorn and disappointment. He had frequently been the disgusted spectator of such scenes, for there was hardly a girl in the neighbourhood who had not been, at some time or other, the only girl whom Robert had ever loved. William was turning contemptuously away when an idea struck him. Perhaps the girl's father was a general or admiral or something, and Robert was worming his secrets out of the daughter. That was a good idea. He brightened and, making his way back to the road, hung about watching the front door. Soon it opened and the younger daughter—a girl of thirteen—came out eating an apple. She was a large sturdy girl and wore her hair in two long plaits.

"Hello," said William in a propitiatory manner.

She looked at him dispassionately and took another bite at her apple without answering.

"I say, it's nice for you having a father in the army," went on William, with what he fondly imagined to be a master-stroke of finesse.

The girl took another bite and still stared at him without answering.

"Oh, I believe it's the navy he's in, isn't it?" went on William.

She removed a small caterpillar from her apple in silence then went on eating.

"Now I come to think of it," said William, "I believe I heard he was in the air force?"

The girl took another bite before answering. Then she said:

"Dad's a dentist. And if you don't stop hanging about our front gate like that he'll come and pull your teeth out for you."

William shuddered. He'd spent an afternoon at the dentist's the week before and the memory was an embittering one.

The girl finished the apple with one large bite and took another from her pocket.

"You buzz off," she said, as she inserted her teeth into it. "No one wants you here. My dad's got his drill with him an'——"

But William was already turning the corner of the road. Out of sight of the house, he slackened his pace, putting his hand to his mouth to make sure all his teeth were there. Having satisfied himself that they were, he gave his whole mind to considering the situation. The affair had, so far, been very disappointing. Still, he was loath to give up his suspicion entirely and decided to make a thorough search of Robert's bedroom. Finding no one about, he made his way there immediately on reaching home and set to work at once to go through all his possessions.

The drawer of his writing-desk was full of papers, and William thought at first that he had at last found the incriminating evidence he was looking for, but, after studying them for some time he realised that the almost illegible scrawl that covered so many sheets was abortive attempts at poems in praise of the beloved, and that what he had at first taken for the plan of an aerodrome was really an attempt at a sketch of the beloved's profile. He replaced them carefully. William's "carefulness" however was at best nothing very great and his fingers were in their usual condition. He next went to Ethel's bedroom. He knew that beautiful women were generally spies, and though he did not consider Ethel beautiful he was aware that many people did. In the bottom of her wardrobe was a box of chocolates and William sampled one tentatively in order to find out if they were poisoned. (A spy might quite conceivably send poisoned chocolates to people in order to get them out of the way.) Finding that they were not, he went on eating them absent-mindedly till the box was empty. He then turned over Ethel's hats in order to see that no treasonable matter was concealed beneath them, replacing them carefully in their right order, not realising that on the delicate surface of each was left the grimy impression of his fingers.

He examined her drawers without much better result, turned over her scarves and gloves and collars, upset a box of powder by mistake, experimented with her rouge and spilt some on to her dressing-table cover, upset a bottle of eau-de-Cologne and filled it up with water, noting with interest that it seemed to turn to milk, and then went quietly out again, fondly imagining that Ethel would never realise that her things had been disturbed. These two disappointments somewhat dulled his zest and he would probably have forgotten all about the spy question, had not the next half-holiday been wet and had he not gone with Ginger to the pictures at Hadley. William was not really fond of the pictures, but this time one of the films held him spellbound from beginning to end. It was about a spy—a large fat spy with a round jolly face and a jovial manner. He wore spectacles and had a head that was completely bald except just at the back. He was very popular and no one dreamt that he was a spy. All William's vague suspicions leapt to life once more.

"I bet they're everywhere—all over the place," he said to Ginger as they went home. "Stands to reason they are. I bet all those jolly sort of people you meet are really spies. They get a lot of money for it, too. Shouldn't be surprised if that dentist isn't one. There isn't any *proof* he's a dentist. She only *said* so, an' she looked just as if she was goin' to grow up a spy. I bet she jus' eats apples to make it look like as if she wasn't one. An' there's Robert goin' there every day. I bet they're either trainin' him to be a spy or gettin' his secrets out of him somehow."

But he couldn't really convince himself that Robert had any secrets worth getting out, or that Robert himself was a spy, for Robert was obviously going through yet another of those affairs of the heart whose emotional intensity never seemed to be dulled by repetition. No, he couldn't seriously suspect Robert of being a spy, and he couldn't really suspect the dentist or the dentist's daughter, either, though he tried very hard. He'd met the dentist in the village, and he'd looked so exactly like a dentist that even William couldn't suspect him of being anything else. Still, he decided to keep his eyes open. Sometimes his father brought men home to dinner. Any one of them might turn out to be a spy. He'd look out for fat bald men with jovial manners. Ginger promised to do the same. Ginger was not much interested in spies, but he was always ready to oblige William.

"Our gardener's fat an' bald," he said, "but I don't think he's a spy."

"*Anyone* can be a spy," said William sternly. "If you start sayin' people can't be spies you'll never catch one. You keep your eye on him, anyway. I'm goin' to keep my eye on everyone I know—even the Vicar an' suchlike. He might have jus' set up as a clergyman to put people off the scent."

Ginger promised to keep his eye on the gardener in particular and everyone else in general and the two parted.

William went home very thoughtfully, his mind once more filled with suspicion of his fellow-creatures.

His mother greeted him absently, and William wondered whether or no to include her among his suspects. After all, why not? She appeared to be a busy wife and mother, but that might be a blind, and she might all the time be discovering secrets and sending them off to foreign countries. Thinking the matter over, however, he couldn't imagine what secrets she could discover, nor to whom she could send them, so rather reluctantly he crossed her off his list.

"William, dear," she said as he sat down to have his tea, "I do hope you'll be on your best behaviour this evening. A friend of your father is coming to dinner. It's a very important visit and your father particularly wants you to behave well."

William groaned. He knew the dullness of these important visitors and the gulf that yawned between his conception of good behaviour and that of other people.

"Who is the chap, anyway?" put in Robert, who was standing in front of the mantelpiece studying his reflection in the mirror and trying to solve the eternal problem of whether he was good looking or not.

"He's a Mr. Fletcher, dear," said Mrs. Brown. "I don't understand business, of course, but it seems he's a director of the Dodo Copper Mine in Rhodesia and they've struck a very rich deposit of copper or something. He's letting just a few people have shares in it, and a friend of your father's on the Stock Exchange has persuaded him to come and have a talk with your father."

"I bet he's a spy," said William, with his mouth full of bread and jam.

"Shut up," snapped Robert.

"So you see it's a very important visit," went on Mrs. Brown, "because it's very lucky indeed for your father that he's been put in touch with this man."

But they weren't listening to her. William was thinking that perhaps the window-cleaner would be a good person to shadow as having plenty of opportunity of finding out secrets, and Robert was wondering whether the gardener or his mother would notice if he took some fuchsias from the greenhouse to present to the beloved.

William, in fact, was just on the point of sallying forth to the cottage where the window-cleaner lived in order to watch him and see if he was engaged in treasonable correspondence with some foreign government when the visitor was announced, and at once he lost interest in everything else. For the visitor was a large fat man with a round jolly face and a jovial manner. He wore spectacles and had a head that was completely bald except just at the back. One look at him, in fact, told William that here was the villain of the picture miraculously come to life. William's eyes gleamed as he shook hands with him. Here was the arch spy of the whole world under his own roof. He must make the most of the time at his disposal. It would be terrible if he let his prey escape him now that he had him in his grasp. He glanced over his adversary's person. He probably had some of his stolen plans concealed on him somewhere. That pocket looked rather bulky, so did that one, and he carried an attaché case. He wished he had a revolver. People in films who were after spies always had revolvers. He'd have to be very careful, of course. The spy in the picture had stuck at nothing. The visitor greeted Mrs. Brown and William, then went into the study with Mr. Brown. William hung about outside the door, feeling baulked and discomfited. How could he prove that he was a spy and bring him to justice if he couldn't even hear what he was saying? He looked about him cautiously. The coast was quite clear. His mother was knitting in the drawing-room. Ethel and Robert were out. (Robert had decided on a bold course and had taken all the fuchsias as well as most of the begonias.) In the kitchen the maids were busy with the dinner. William advanced to the study door and applied his ear to the keyhole. Isolated phrases reached him in the visitor's fat unctuous voice.

"Only too happy to let you in on the shares . . . same belt, probably, as other Rhodesian mines but much richer . . . let you in at par . . . immediate funds necessary for machinery, etc. . . . . No time to put them on the open market . . . naturally wish friends of my friends to have first chance. These one pound shares will, in a year's time, be worth, at least, twenty pounds . . ."

William's face grew longer and longer. This was just business—and very dull business at that. The fat man evidently wasn't a spy, after all. He still went on listening without much interest. Mr. Brown was suggesting thinking the matter over. The visitor demurred. After to-morrow not a single share would be left. He still had two more friends to see and they would certainly snap up what were left. There was a little more conversation, then William applied his eye to the keyhole and saw his father write out a cheque and hand it to the visitor. He was turning away in disgust when a phrase arrested his attention.

"Don't forget, Mr. Brown, I'm letting you in on the ground floor. This is your great opportunity. America is already interested. There is a ready market there."

William gave a gasp of excitement. The man was a spy. He was, moreover, persuading his father to be his accomplice, saying that he would let him in to the ground floor of some government building—through a window probably—to steal some plans, which they were then going to sell to America. William's eyes grew rounder and rounder with horror as all the implications of what he had heard dawned on him. His father was in the hands of this villain and must be saved at all costs. He heard the drawing-room door open and his mother come out. William at once pretended to be deeply engrossed in the umbrella-stand.

"What are you doing, William?" said Mrs. Brown.

"I'm jus' wonderin' whether I could make one of these," said William with great cunning. "I bet I could with a saw an' a bit of wood."

"Well, it's your bedtime, dear," said his mother, "so never mind about that now. Go to bed very quietly, because I don't want your father disturbed. He's having a most important talk."

William snorted. She'd have a jolly fright if she knew what the talk was about, if she knew that the visitor was not only a spy himself but had actually succeeded in persuading her husband to get through the ground-floor window of the War Office to steal some plans and sell them to America.

He went slowly upstairs, still snorting ironically to himself.

"Mind you clean your teeth properly," said Mrs. Brown.

William leant over the baluster.

"I've got other things to think of than teeth," he said darkly. "I bet I could tell you somethin' that'd drive teeth clean out of your head."

But Mrs. Brown had vanished into the kitchen to supervise the final preparations of the dinner.

William went upstairs and waited till he heard the sounds of his mother, father and the guest going into the dining-room. When the coast was at last clear he crept downstairs to the hall. Yes, there was the guest's attaché case on the floor just by the hat-stand. He snatched it up, crept back to his room again and, shutting the door, sat down on the floor to examine the contents. They were disappointing. Letters about copper and pyrites and copper sulphide and copies of meaningless telegrams. Nothing to be learnt there, thought William with a sigh, as he tossed them on one side. The examination had taken some time, and downstairs dinner was just over. The guest was evidently in a hurry. He could not, it seemed, even stay for coffee. No, business . . . business . . . always business, he said with his fat unctuous laugh. His case? His case . . . There was general confusion as everyone began to hunt for his case. They searched the hall and study and dining-room and drawing-room. The guest's unctuous laugh grew a trifle less unctuous and a note of anxiety invaded it. A sudden idea struck Mr. Brown. He went upstairs to William's room. William was on his knees in the act of bundling the papers back into the case. He turned to meet his father's eye.

"Give me that at once," said Mr. Brown sternly, and added on a sinister note: "I'll deal with you later, my boy."

"But listen, father," protested William, "it was like this . . . You see . . ."

But Mr. Brown had snatched up the case and descended the stairs. William heard him explaining to the guest that the case had been taken upstairs by mistake, heard with a sinking heart the last genial farewells and the closing of the front door, then, with a heart that sank deeper still, the sound of his father's footsteps briskly ascending the stairs. As he entered William's bedroom, his face wore the look against which, William knew, protestations and pleadings and excuses were vain. Retribution was inevitable, and the only thing to do was just to yield to the storm and get it over as soon as possible.

"Disgraceful!" Mr. Brown was saying. "Utterly disgraceful! Prying into the possessions of a guest in your own house! Have you no sense of honour? You need a lesson, my boy, and I'm going to give you one you won't forget in a hurry." His eye was caught by a piece of paper just under William's bed. He stooped and picked it up. It was one of the meaningless telegrams, which William in his haste had omitted to put back into the case. "This, I suppose, is one of his papers. It may be a most important one. He may be suffering serious inconvenience from the loss of it, and all because my son—*my son*—is so devoid of a sense of honour as to——'' His voice died away. He was studying the paper with interest. "In code, of course," he murmured, then, remembering William's presence, added: "Disgraceful! Utterly disgraceful." It was obvious, however, that the mysterious telegram interested him at the moment far more than William. "I'll just see if Bentley——" He went from the room abruptly and down the staircase. William felt that the safest thing to do would be to stay where he was and hope that his father would forget him, but curiosity vanquished discretion and he finally followed his father down to his study. There Mr. Brown, taking a large book from the shelves and turning over the pages, began to work out the code of the telegram. Soon, on the clean piece of paper he had taken for the purpose, appeared the words:

Dodo. N. Rhodesia. Regret Inform Samples Assays Confirm Deposit Petered Out Diamond Drills Proof Conclusive No Hope Restrike Stop Await Your Cabled Advice When Make Failure Public.

Just as he wrote the last word Mrs. Brown appeared. She had heard Mr. Brown plunge upstairs then plunge downstairs and had just waited till she'd finished turning her heel before coming to investigate. She still carried her knitting and knitted placidly as she spoke.

"What's the matter, dear?" she said.

"Matter?" shouted Mr. Brown furiously. "The matter is that I've been stung. Or rather that I should have been stung if you hadn't had a rascal and ruffian for a son. Thank Heaven there's time to stop the cheque." He tried to assume an expression of severity. He looked at William. "Let this be a lesson to you, my boy. I mean,

"LET THIS BE A LESSON TO YOU, MY BOY," SAID MR. BROWN.

it's turned out all right this time, as it happens, so I'll say
no more about it, but——"

Robert and Ethel entered tumultuously. They hadn't
found the traces of William's investigations till just before dinner, and the presence of the guest had prevented

"MY HATS ARE RUINED," DECLARED ETHEL, CRYING.

their taking any counter action. Now they had come to lay their complaint before Authority. Their indignation had not suffered any diminution in the interval. They fixed accusing eyes on the culprit as they began their indignant chorus.

"He's been into *all* my things," said Ethel.

"My most *private* papers," said Robert.

"There simply isn't *anything* he's not messed about and left upside down," said Ethel.

"Marks all over my collars," said Robert.

"My hats *ruined*," said Ethel. "Filthy finger-marks all over everything."

They stopped, looking sternly from William to his father and waiting with complacent certainty for Nemesis to overtake the culprit.

Mr. Brown looked up absently from the telegram.

"Wash your hands before you do it again, my boy," he said mildly to William. "People don't like dirty finger-marks on their things."

Robert and Ethel stared at him, open-mouthed with astonishment. Not thus was Authority accustomed to receive their complaints.

"But, father——" they began simultaneously.

"Yes, yes, yes," said Mr. Brown testily. "I heard what you said. Run along now, children. I'm very busy. I have to ring up the bank manager."

William had gathered breath to enter into one of his lengthy self-justifications, but he let it out again. He didn't understand in the least bit what had happened, but he did understand that retribution seemed to have been miraculously averted from him. It was probably a mistake, and he'd better make the most of it before it was discovered. The best thing to do was to go to bed and to sleep quickly. No one could do anything to him if he was in bed and asleep.

"But I don't understand," said Mrs. Brown. "Do tell us what's happened, dear."

Mr. Brown told them in a few short pungent words what had happened.

"How clever of William!" said Mrs. Brown, dropping a stitch and dexterously picking it up again.

"Clever!" snorted Robert and Ethel simultaneously.

"Tell me, dear," began Mrs. Brown, looking round for William.

But William wasn't there. He was in bed and asleep.

Chapter 4

A Few Dogs and William

WILLIAM picked up the large greyish object and examined it carefully.

"I say! A mushroom!" he announced.

The others looked at it doubtfully.

"Bet it's a toadstool," said Ginger. "There's been people killed eatin' 'em thinkin' they were mushrooms."

"Well, I bet this *is* a mushroom," persisted William. "I'm goin' to take it home an' ask them to cook it. I'll give it my mother for a present. That's a jolly good idea. It's her birthday nex' week."

"A mushroom won't count," said Douglas. "Not for a birthday. They don't."

" 'Sides," added Ginger, "I bet it's a toadstool. I c'n tell by the colour. A mushroom's sort of white."

"Well, this is sort of white," said William.

"Well, a mushroom's sort of whiter. It's not so flat, either. It's got a sort of round top."

"Well, so has this."

"Well, go on, then. Eat it an' see if you die," challenged Ginger.

"No, I don't like 'em raw," said William. "I'm goin' to get it cooked."

"I bet no one'll cook it for you. They'll jus' throw it in the dust-bin an' tell you not to come botherin' them."

This sounded so probable that William did not contradict it.

"I'll cook it myself, then," he said. "I'll light a fire an' cook it on a stick."

"You'll die if it's a toadstool," Ginger warned him again, "an' I bet you anythin' it is."

William smelled it and licked it tentatively.

"It's a mushroom all right," he said, but he spoke less certainly.

They had reached the road and were passing Miss Tressider's house. Miss Tressider was an elderly, cantankerous, short-sighted lady who owned an elderly, cantankerous, short-sighted Yorkshire terrier called Nero. Nero was standing at the gate now and growled softly at the Outlaws as they passed, more on general principles than because it had anything against them. William stopped. He liked to be on friendly terms with the canine population of the village, and the growl was a challenge.

"Hi, boy!" he said in a conciliatory tone.

Nero growled again.

William held out the hand that contained the dubious mushroom and said "Hi, boy!" again. Nero advanced, smelt the offering, and suddenly, before any of them could stop him, swallowed it.

"Gosh!" said William dismayed.

"Crumbs!" said Ginger. 'I jolly well hope it *was* a mushroom."

"Come away, quick," said Douglas apprehensively, " 'fore she sees us. She'll say it's our fault if it dies. She'll kick up an awful fuss."

They went down the road quickly and in silence.

"I bet it *was* a mushroom," said William at last, anxiously. "Anyway, I didn't mean it to eat it."

"They won't b'lieve you didn't," said Douglas gloomily. "Not if it dies. She thinks an awful lot of it. I bet she'll write to our fathers an' start kickin' up a row."

"Anyway, I'm pretty sure it *was* a mushroom," said William.

He went home and was very thoughtful during lunch, refusing a third helping of pudding out of sheer absent-mindedness.

During the afternoon he tried to forget the episode, but the memory of it nagged uneasily at his mind, as he issued orders to his braves in the character of a Red Indian chief or made ferocious wild beasts obey his nod in the character of a lion-tamer.

And at tea-time the bomb fell.

"I met Miss Tressider in the village," said Ethel carelessly. "The poor old thing was in such a state. That dog of hers is dead."

William swallowed half a bun unmasticated.

"W-what?" he stammered.

"I wasn't talking to you," said Ethel distantly

William stared at her, his face blank with horror. It must have been a toadstool, after all. . . .

Ethel went on to talk of other local affairs. Evidently no one connected him with the death of the dog. That, at any rate, was a relief. But not much of one, for the fact remained that he was responsible. He'd held out a toadstool as if it were some appetising dainty, and Nero, trusting him blindly, had eaten it. The brand of Cain seemed to descend on him. He rose from the table with a muttered excuse. His mother looked at him in amazement, for he had done less than justice to his notoriously healthy appetite.

"Don't you want any more tea, William?" she said.

"No, thanks," said William.

"Have you a headache, dear?" she said solicitously.

William laughed harshly.

A headache! Fancy asking anyone if they'd a headache when they'd just murdered a dog! Showed how little anyone understood. Here he was with a horrible crime like that on his conscience and she asked him if he'd got a headache! He enjoyed the sound of his harsh laugh and did it again.

"It seems to me like a stomach cough, dear," said his mother, still mildly solicitous. "I'd better give you a dose to-night."

He changed the laugh into a snort and went out into the hall. There he stood, scowling ferociously at the hat-stand and considering the situation. He'd murdered Miss Tressider's dog. The next step was obvious. He must get her another. Having come to this conclusion, he turned his mind to his financial resources. He had just sixpence-halfpenny. He didn't know much about the price of dogs, but he thought that you ought to be able to get quite a good one for sixpence-halfpenny. Sixpence-halfpenny was, after all, a pretty large sum of money. It was, indeed, an unusual chance that he possessed it. The sixpence had been given him by an aunt who'd been to tea yesterday and had been so agreeably surprised to find him out (he'd been having tea at Ginger's) that in a moment of expansive relief she had left sixpence for him with his mother. The halfpenny had been earned in much the same way from Ethel for being in his bedroom and out of the way when some new and rather grand friends came to call for her in their Rolls-Royce. (She could not know, of course, that he had occupied himself by pulling faces at an embarrassed chauffeur from his bedroom window.)

He took the two coins out of his pocket and looked at

them regretfully. He'd meant to buy a pistol with them. There was a large and splendid-looking pistol in the window of the village shop marked sixpence-halfpenny. But it would have to wait now. It was his imperative duty to buy another dog for Miss Tressider. There was a dog shop in Hadley, he remembered. He'd go there at once, and he'd get a dog as like as possible to the one that had eaten the toadstool. He was glad that Jumble was entirely unlike Nero and also that Miss Tressider disliked him and referred to him as "that dreadful mongrel." It would have been terrible if he'd had to give up Jumble.

As he emerged from the front door Jumble greeted him tempestuously, wagging his collie tail, cocking his fox-terrier ears, sniffing joyously with his retriever nose, his dachshund body a-quiver with the anticipation of a walk with William in the wood.

William looked at him wistfully. It would have been jolly to take Jumble into Hadley with him (Jumble was always so enraptured with life, so certain that everything was going to turn out for the best, that it was impossible to remain depressed in his presence), but he would be sure to run riot in the dog shop. He'd try to make friends with the wrong dogs and it would end in a fight. Jumble had almost as great a genius as his master for precipitating a crisis with the best intentions in the world. No, he'd leave Jumble at home till he'd finally fixed up this dog business.

"I can't take you with me, Jumble," he said sadly. "I'm doin' somethin' very important."

He took Jumble round to the back of the house, found a clothes-line that someone had left on the lawn, and tied him up with it to the summer-house. Then he set off for Hadley. Having reached the dog shop, he stood looking in at the window. The exhibits were mostly small white puppies. He watched their antics for a few minutes, so much absorbed that he quite forgot the serious business on which he had come. Then he remembered, frowned purposefully, felt in his pocket to make sure that the sixpence-halfpenny was still there, and entered the shop. A small stout supercilious-looking man, rather like a Pekinese, came forward.

"I want a big brown dog, please," said William. "A sort of Yorkshire terrier."

The man winced slightly at the "sort of".

"We only keep pedigree dogs here," he said.

"Yes, that's the sort I meant," said William easily.

The man looked at him doubtfully. This small grubby boy did not look like the potential purchaser of a pedigree dog, but one couldn't be certain of anything with the modern child.

He led the way to the back of the shop and opened a large kennel. A brown dog strolled out. William's heart leapt. It was the very double of Miss Tressider's late pet.

"How much is it?" he said casually, fingering his two coins affectionately and hoping that it wouldn't be *quite* sixpence-halfpenny. Even if it were sixpence it would leave a halfpenny to buy some sweets on the way home. Liquorice allsorts weighed light and you got quite a lot for a halfpenny. On the other hand, Jumble didn't like liquorice, and it seemed rather mean to get something that Jumble didn't like. So perhaps he'd better get humbugs. Jumble liked humbugs.

"Ten pounds," said the man.

With a tremendous effort William concealed his emotion.

"Oh . . . " he said, then glanced disparagingly at the

"HOW MUCH IS IT?" ASKED WILLIAM.

brown dog. "He's not quite the sort I want," he went on nonchalantly. "What other sorts have you?"

The man displayed the remainder of his wares. William felt dizzy as the prices soared up to twenty and thirty pounds, but he managed to maintain his aloof disparaging expression.

"What's the cheapest you have?" he asked at length.

The man returned to the shop and took up the smallest of the white puppies.

"I'd sell this for five pounds," he said, "because of its tail. It's dirt cheap, of course."

William would have liked to reply "of course", but felt too dizzy. Dirt cheap. Five *pounds*. *Gosh!*

"No," he said at last, managing with great difficulty to sound slightly hesitating. "No, I don't think that's jus' what I want either." He looked round him. "There's nothin' here jus' what I want. Well, thanks very much. Good afternoon."

He walked out of the shop and down the street, trying not to look as if he were beating an ignominious retreat. The Pekinese man watched him suspiciously. What was the little devil up to?

Out of sight, William leant against a wall to recover. Twenty ... thirty pounds ... *Crumbs!* Well, he couldn't buy one. That much was certain. He'd have to get one some other way. And suddenly another idea occurred to him. He remembered hearing that poor people often turned their dogs out of doors in order to avoid paying the licence. He'd find a dog that had been turned out of doors to avoid paying the licence and take it to Miss Tressider. He wandered about the streets for some time trying to find a dog that had been turned out of doors to avoid paying the licence but was soon brought up against the difficulties of the task. Even if one found a dog wandering about by itself, how could one be sure that it had actually been turned out of doors? Another idea struck him. He must find a family of poor people and offer to take their dog off their hands to save them paying the licence. That would be quite plain sailing, and there wouldn't be any possibility of mistake. He must find a poor family with a brown dog. He began to wander about the back streets of the town. Luck seemed to be with him, for he soon found a long lean brown dog with a foolish expression and one ear shorter than the other. It was, of course, not strikingly like the victim of the toadstool tragedy, but it was brown and about the same size and, to William's optimistic eye, seemed eminently suitable for his purpose. While he was in the act of inspecting it, it turned and walked into a small cottage near. That was evidently its home. All he had to do, then, was to follow it and offer to relieve its owners of it, so that they wouldn't have to pay its licence. He felt a strange and unaccountable nervousness, but soon mastered it and, crossing over to the half-open door, knocked softly. An old woman opened it and stared at him suspiciously.

"We don't want nothin'," she announced, "an' we've got nothin' for you. So you can jus' go back where you came from."

"Who is it, Ma?" called a voice from the inner room.

"It's a boy," said the old woman. "Reg'lar little varmint, 'e looks, too."

A woman came out of the inner room, drying her face on a towel. She looked at William aggressively.

"If you've come tellin' tales about our 'Erbert," she said, "I'll give you somethin' to take 'ome with you. An' don't you say you didn't 'it 'im first 'cause I know you did. Always starting the trouble an' then comin' round to complain of our 'Erbert . . ."

William, too much disconcerted at first by his reception to speak, now found his tongue.

"No," he said reassuringly, as he entered the small room. "I've—I've come about the dog, that's all."

" 'Itler?" said the woman still more aggressively. "Well, what's 'e done to you? If you start fooling round with 'im 'course 'e'll bite you. An' if you say 'e's taken one of your Ma's chickens, well, I'll want proof, that's all. People didn't oughter keep chickens in the town, wakin' folks up all night. An' why 'asn't yer Ma come 'erself—sendin' a silly kid like you?"

A large man had now come into the room. He wore an open shirt and a muffler and a few days' growth of beard. He looked truculent and very very strong. William began to wish that he'd chosen some other poor family, but he couldn't draw back now.

"What's all this 'ere?" said the man scowling.

"This kid's come round to say that 'Itler's 'ad one of his Ma's chickens," said the old woman.

Hitler, who was sitting on the hearthrug, turned round with a foolish grin at the sound of his name.

"No, I haven't," said William, managing at last to make his voice heard. "I didn't say that."

"That's right," said the old woman. "Call me a liar to me face. I know what I'd do to you if I was your Ma, cheeky little varmint."

She made a threatening gesture at him as she spoke and William felt an overwhelming desire to turn tail and flee, but he remembered Nero and the toadstool and stood his ground.

"It's about the licence," he said. "The dog licence for the dog."

He stopped helplessly. The room had now become full of children who seemed to have sprung up from nowhere, but who were obviously part of the family. A child of eighteen months or so was sitting on the floor at his feet, laboriously unfastening his shoe-laces. Another was pummelling at him from behind. Others were making loud and uncomplimentary remarks about his personal appearance. Hitler sat in the background, surveying the scene with his foolish grin.

"THAT'S RIGHT," SAID THE OLD WOMAN. "CALL ME A LIAR TO ME FACE."

"I know what it is," said the old woman at last, triumphantly. "'E's come from one of them there Sercities what pay folks' dog licences for 'em. Fancy sendin' a batty kid like that? Oughter be ashamed of themselves. Well, where is it? Come on. Seven an' six it oughter be, an' if you've pinched any of it . . ."

"Charity!" spat out the man. "I'm sick of their blasted charity. Come on," he said to William. " 'And it over, can't you?"

Desperation made William articulate at last.

"I've not got the axshul money for the licence," he said, "but I thought it'd be jus' as good if I took the dog off you so's you wouldn't have to pay its licence. I'll take it with me now an'——"

But he got no farther.

The entire family seemed to rise up and fall upon him with one accord, and in a few seconds he found himself sitting on the pavement outside, his coat half off, his collar hanging open, his tie missing and his whole body one large bruise. He picked himself up and hurried away as quickly as he could.

At the corner of the street he turned and looked back. It was empty except for Hitler, who stood gazing after him with his foolish smile. He drew on his coat, fastened his collar, and set off homewards.

So far his efforts to find a substitute for the unfortunate Nero had been singularly unsuccessful, but that only increased his determination. There must be a way if he could only think of it. He stood silent and motionless, staring at the passing traffic, and—suddenly thought of it. Miss Mortimer. She lived at Marleigh, and she possessed three dogs, one of which—Hereward—was a Yorkshire terrier exactly like Nero. He wouldn't have taken it, he assured himself, if it had been her only dog, but she had three and Miss Tressider now had none. It was quite fair. He'd tried to solve the problem in an honest law-abiding fashion. It was no fault of his that he was now driven by fate to other means. He'd take Miss

Mortimer's dog and tie it up in Nero's empty kennel.
Miss Mortimer would still have two dogs, which was
enough for anyone, and so everyone would be quite satisfied. William assured himself most emphatically on the
last point, determinedly shutting his eyes to any other
aspect of the affair. Everyone would be quite satisfied.

Having made his decision, he wasted no further time.
He crossed the road (causing two motorists to jam on
their brakes and curse him roundly, and giving one old
lady a heart attack) and made his way quickly up to
Marleigh to Miss Mortimer's house. Luck seemed to be
with him again. Hereward stood just inside the gate,
looking bored and friendly, and no one else was about.
William made tentative overtures of friendship.
Hereward responded. William walked slowly down the
road, saying "Hi, boy!" over his shoulder in his most
persuasive tones. Hereward hesitated for a moment and
then began to follow, wagging his tail as if to intimate
that he was quite willing to be William's dog for a time if
William wanted him. William stooped down and, taking
the lace from one of his shoes, used it as a lead, but there
was really no need of it. Hereward was evidently ready
to follow wherever fate, in the person of William, led.
William led him round to the back of Miss Tressider's
garden and fastened him to a chain by Nero's kennel,
then, his duty done, his task fulfilled, set off homeward
with a light step.

But Hereward realised suddenly that he'd been
betrayed. He'd thought he was going for a walk with a
boy. He liked boys. They were adventurous and high-
spirited and incalculable, and Miss Mortimer was none
of these things. He'd belonged to a boy before he
belonged to Miss Mortimer, and when he set off with
William he was looking forward to an hour or two of the

old adventurous life before settling down again to his spinsterish routine with Miss Mortimer. Instead, he found himself chained up beside a strange kennel. Hereward was not a dog to suffer in silence. He lifted up his head and howled desolately. Miss Tressider came to the window and stared at him, blenching. She'd been sorrowing for poor dear Nero and had just said, "If only he could come back to me for one hour, just for one hour . . ." when those unearthly howls rent the air, and—there he was sitting by his kennel just as he used to, though she'd seen him buried with her own eyes only that morning. He'd never howled like that in his lifetime, of course, but that only made the whole thing more impressive. His spirit had come back to her with some message. It was trying to tell her something. She opened the window and leaned out, trembling.

"Nero," she said. "What is it, Nero?"

Hereward continued to howl. He was trying to tell the whole world that a boy had promised him a crowded hour of glorious life and then basely deserted him. He'd rather have even Miss Mortimer—dull as she was—than this.

"Nero," said Miss Tressider again. "Oh, Nero, what is it?"

Hereward continued to howl. Then Miss Tressider remembered Miss Bullamore. Miss Bullamore (on the strength of possessing a handbook on palmistry) did the fortune telling at all the local fêtes and was generally supposed to be psychic. Perhaps she'd be able to interpret Nero's howls. She lived over at Marleigh, but it wouldn't take long to reach Marleigh on her bicycle. She leant out of the window again. The howls still rent the air.

"I'll be back soon, Nero, dear," she said tremulously,

"and then, perhaps, I'll be able to understand your message."

Hereward rolled an angry eye in her direction and threw back his head with an even more resonant howl.

Still trembling, Miss Tressider flung on her hat and got out her bicycle. Her hat was over one ear and her back tyre was almost flat, but she didn't care. She didn't care for anything but getting dear Nero's message translated as quickly as possible.

Miss Bullamore was interested, but slightly distrait, for Miss Mortimer had just paid her a visit in deep distress. Hereward had disappeared. He'd been standing at the gate one minute (she'd seen him distinctly from the window) and the next he'd disappeared. Simply disappeared. She was certain it was thieves. He was a valuable dog, and she'd always been afraid of his getting stolen. No one but a thief could have spirited him away so completely, leaving no trace at all. He had too sweet a nature . . . he was too trusting . . . and Heaven only knew what he'd do without her. No one but she understood the exact temperature he liked his bread and milk at night. She'd rung up the police, of course, but they were no use. She begged Miss Bullamore to use her psychic powers in order to discover where he was. Miss Bullamore tried but without success. In spite of the handbook on palmistry, her psychic powers were somewhat uncertain. They worked best after the event. When anything had happened Miss Bullamore often impressed her friends by saying that she'd had a "feeling" that it was going to. . . .

Miss Mortimer begged her to have a "feeling" about Hereward, but Miss Bullamore explained that one couldn't have them to order. She told Miss Mortimer to go home and said that she'd try to have one when she was alone. She hoped that Hereward would be found soon and then she could have had a "feeling" that he was there all the time. She was somewhat disconcerted by Miss Tressider's request, but, on the whole, it wasn't too difficult. She'd never had any dealings with spirit dogs before but it ought to be quite easy to interpret its howls. She rather fancied herself at interpreting dreams—she made her interpretations very vague and very beautiful—and this ought to be pretty much the same. Anyway, no one would be able to prove that it didn't mean whatever she said it meant, and that was the chief thing.

"Yes, I'll come at once," she said briskly.

"Will you bring your crystal?" said Miss Tressider.

Miss Bullamore had purchased a crystal the year before, but had never yet succeeded in seeing anything in it but her own reflection.

"No, I don't think a crystal would be quite suitable," she said. "Not for a dog."

"Perhaps not," sighed Miss Tressider.

Miss Bullamore collected her hat and coat and bag.

"I wonder if it would be kind to take Miss Mortimer," she said. "She's just lost Hereward, and it might take her mind off him. On the other hand, of course, it might remind her of him, so perhaps we'd better not."

Miss Tressider agreed and Miss Bullamore got out her bicycle and the two of them cycled down towards Miss Tressider's house.

Meantime William, having put Hereward in Nero's place, walked slowly homeward, pursued by the sounds of those raucous desolate howls. He walked more and more slowly and finally stopped. No, he couldn't possibly give Miss Tressider a dog that howled like that. It was worse than no dog at all. It took a lot to get William's conscience going, but, once going, it took a lot to stop it. He'd undertaken to supply Miss Tressider with a dog in place of the one who'd eaten his toadstool, and he couldn't leave her a dog that howled like that. He wouldn't mind a howling dog himself (he'd rather like one), but experience had taught him that elderly maiden ladies have peculiar ideas about noise. He was passing Mr. Cornish's house. Mr. Cornish had a bull terrier called Oberon, a nice quiet dog who never barked or howled in any circumstances. It was an old dog and had a weak chest, and William had often heard Mr. Cornish say that it was more trouble to him than it was worth. It was just the dog for Miss Tressider and Mr. Cornish would presumably be glad to be relieved of it as it was more trouble to him than it was worth. Miss Tressider wouldn't mind its weak chest. She was always getting colds herself and it could share her medicines.

He made his way cautiously to the back of Mr. Cornish's house. Oberon, large, whitish pink and ungainly, sat by his kennel. He squirmed ecstatically when he saw William and made a clumsy leap in his direction. One of Oberon's delusions was that he was still a puppy, and he liked to pretend to gambol after stones and sticks, though he was almost too short-sighted to see them. William unfastened the chain and threw an imaginary stick down the drive. Oberon lumbered after it, wheezing joyfully. William repeated the action. Oberon sported heavily along the road, seeing himself as a puppy out with a boy, making elephantine runs and rushes at nothing in particular. Blindly trusting, he accompanied William in at the gate of Miss Tressider's house and round to the back, where Hereward was still filling the air with his lamentations. It was the work of a few seconds to undo Hereward and fasten

Oberon to the chain. Hereward wasted no time demanding explanations but vanished like a streak of lightning into the distance. Oberon sat down heavily, thumping his tail on the ground. He'd had a tiring walk and was glad to be chained up. Free, he'd have felt it incumbent on him to go on pretending to be a puppy, so he was quite glad not to be free. William looked down at him speculatively. He seemed happy, and anyway he couldn't howl because he wheezed so much that he could hardly bark. Yes, he'd do beautifully for Miss Tressider's new dog. Having come to this conclusion, William, feeling that he'd spent quite enough time on the business, set off homeward once more.

*   *   *

Miss Tressider sat down weakly on a chair near the door.

"He's stopped howling," she said. "Do see if he's still there, dear. I'm so shaken by the whole thing that I simply daren't. I don't really know whether he's visible to anyone else, but, of course, you'll be able to see him because you're psychic."

Miss Bullamore, putting on her psychic look, went to the window.

"Yes, I can see him," she said triumphantly.

"What's he doing, dear?" said Miss Tressider faintly.

"Just sitting."

"Not pulling at the chain or howling or anything?"

"No. Just sitting. Just a white dog sitting. That's all I see."

"*White?*" screamed Miss Tressider. "Has he gone *white?*" She dropped her face in her hands. "Oh, my poor Nero. I can't bear to look. Does—does he look like a ghost? He must, of course, if he's gone white. Is he—is he fading away?"

Miss Bullamore gazed at the solid form of Oberon.

"No, dear. He doesn't seem to be fading away."

"Can you tell what he's trying to say?" quavered Miss Tressider.

But at that moment Miss Mortimer arrived. She was angry and breathless. She'd been told that Hereward was in Miss Tressider's back garden, that Miss Tressider, in fact, having lost her Nero, had basely kidnapped Hereward. A small boy, who had seen him through the hedge, had hastened to Miss Mortimer with the news. He was quite sure it was Hereward. Anyway, it couldn't be Nero because Nero was dead. Miss Mortimer had set off at once to investigate the story. She demanded to see the dog that was tied up to Miss Tressider's kennel.

"I'm afraid you won't be able to see him, dear," said Miss Tressider sadly, "because you aren't psychic. Besides, he's fading away. He's gone white and stopped howling in the last half-hour. He isn't your Hereward, but I can't really explain, because it's all so mysterious and occult. Miss Bullamore has come to try and interpret it. Stand aside, dear, and let Miss Mortimer look."

Miss Bullamore stood away from the window, and the three of them gazed at the plump solid figure of Oberon, who wheezed at them in greeting and thumped his tail on the ground.

"It's not Nero," gasped Miss Tressider.

"Well, it's certainly not Hereward," said Miss Mortimer, losing interest in the situation. "What liars children are!"

"Let's go out to him," suggested Miss Bullamore, who was feeling relieved that she hadn't risked her psychic reputation by interpreting Nero's message.

They were just on the point of following her advice when Mr. Cornish arrived. Mr. Cornish, as small and peppery as Oberon was large and placid, had been most annoyed to find Oberon gone when he came to take him for his constitutional, and still more annoyed when a passer-by informed him that he'd seen Oberon chained up in Miss Tressider's back garden. Mr. Cornish had come to demand an explanation. He'd never liked Miss Tressider since she'd simply forced him to buy an expensive cushion that he didn't want at the Church Bazaar last summer, but that she should calmly appropriate his dog simply beat everything. He wasn't going to put up with it. If necessary he was prepared to call in the police. He'd given in about the cushion, but he certainly wasn't going to give in about this. A woman who'd behaved like that over the cushion was capable of anything. . . . He'd go to the police this very evening. The presence of Miss Mortimer and Miss Bullamore merely added to his anger. They were all of a piece. Hadn't Miss Bullamore accused him only last spring of copying her arrangement of bulbs in his front garden? And now—stealing his dog! White with fury, he marched up to the kennel, unfastened Oberon, then turned upon the three women.

"You'll hear of this again," he said. "You'll——"

And then several things happened.

William had almost reached home when his conscience once again began to trouble him. A white dog—he oughtn't to have left a white dog in place of Nero. It was far too unlike the original. Moreover, Oberon was old. It wasn't fair to give her an old dog like that. It should have been a young dog and a brown one. A young brown dog. He was passing Jenks's farm. There were several collies there, he knew. One was a young scatterbrain creature called Victoria whom Farmer Jenks was beginning to despair of ever training as a sheep-dog. She'd do all right. She was brown like Nero and young. And it would be a kindness to Farmer Jenks to relieve him of her. William looked cautiously over the gate into the farmyard. Yes, Victoria was there, trying to fraternise with a morose broody hen. William whistled.

"POOR OLD THING," SAID THE HOUSEMAID. 'SHE IS HAVING A DAY
AND NO MISTAKE."

Victoria cocked her ears and looked at him and finally
decided to accompany him wherever he wanted to take
her. She was bored with the hen and didn't want to be
available when it was time to fetch the cows home. She
frisked round him happily along the road till they came

THE OWNERS WERE SHOUTING FRANTICALLY AT THEIR PETS AND
TRYING TO DISENTANGLE THEM.

to Miss Tressider's house. Made reckless by the success of his former visits, William walked boldly round to the back of the house then stopped. The small lawn seemed full of people. Miss Tressider was there and Miss Bullamore was there and Miss Mortimer was there and Mr. Cornish was there. Mr. Cornish was saying:

"You'll hear of this again. You'll——"

It is probable that, alone, Victoria and Oberon would not have fought, that, if Hereward and Jumble had not arrived simultaneously at that moment, the end would have been happy and peaceful—for everyone except, perhaps, William. But Hereward and Jumble arrived at the same moment, both with a grievance against fate and eager to work off the grievance on their fellow-creatures. Hereward had fled to the woods till he had recovered from the worst of his panic. Then he'd gone home, expecting to be made much of and comforted by his mistress. He was annoyed that she wasn't at home and still more annoyed when he tracked her to the scene of his recent humiliation. There was a fat white dog there, too, who was probably the cause of the whole trouble. Having come to that conclusion, Hereward flung himself savagely upon the fat white dog. Victoria, delighted to find a fight ready to hand, joined in it furiously; Jumble (the cook had fetched the clothes-line for a bit of washing and Jumble, freed, had flown to his beloved master), disliking all of them impartially, leapt into the heart of the fray. The four dogs became a mass of growling, snarling, biting fur. Above the uproar the owners (all except William) shouted frantically to their pets and tried to disentangle them. Mr. Cornish got bitten on the ankle and shouted that he'd sue Miss Tressider for assault and Miss Bullamore had one of her "feelings" and went indoors out of harm's way. Miss

Tressider's housemaid came out and stood by William, surveying the scene calmly.

"Pore ole thing!" she said. "She *is* 'aving a day an' no mistake. That there Nero run over this morning . . ."

"*What?*" said William.

" 'Aven't you 'eard?" said the housemaid. "A great big van, it was. Flattened 'im out, pore ole thing! But it wasn't the driver's fault, 'cause I saw it myself. Blew 'is orn like mad, but Nero, 'e was that deaf, pore ole hing!"

William stared at her blankly. Nero had been run over. His death had had nothing to do with the mushroom. (It probably *was* a mushroom, too, after all, he thought triumphantly.) He'd taken all this trouble for nothing. Getting dog after dog after dog for her, when really it hadn't been his fault at all. Well, he'd wasted enough time over the business. He'd go and buy that pistol. Thank goodness he'd still got his sixpence-half-penny. He was jolly glad that there hadn't been a dog for that price at the shop. He'd have felt mad if he'd spent all his money on a new dog. He would wash his hands of the whole thing and go and buy that pistol. It was no use calling Jumble. Jumble never left a fight till there was no one left to fight with.

He walked cheerfully away, his hands in his pockets, quite unmoved by the nightmare sounds of barking, growling, screaming, shouting that were growing to a crescendo in Miss Tressider's garden.

It was nothing to do with him.

It hadn't been the mushroom, after all.

Chapter 5

The Outlaws go A-Mumming

"It's Christmas in four days now," said Ginger.

"I know," said Douglas. "Seems much longer than a year ago since the last one."

"It always does," said William. "That's what's wrong with Christmas. It comes too slow an' goes too quick. It's ridic'lous only havin' one day for Christmas an' then all that long time with nothin'. I think it oughter be a week."

"Or six weeks, same as Lent," suggested Henry.

"Yes, that'd be a jolly good idea," agreed William. "Six weeks of Christmas with presents every day an' holidays all the time. Gosh, yes, I wouldn't mind that."

"An' no relations comin' over for it," said Ginger.

"No, no relations. No aunts or anythin'."

"An' no useful presents," added Douglas, who had had a French Dictionary given him last Christmas and still felt bitter about it.

"No, no useful presents," they agreed in unison.

Having thus reformed Christmas, they were silent, considering their handiwork with a cheerfulness that gradually faded as they returned to the world of cold facts.

"Well, we aren't likely to get any of it," said William

gloomily. "I bet it'll go on bein' jus' one day an' all relations an' pencil-boxes an' ties an'——"

"——an' French Dictionaries," put in Douglas.

"Yes, an' French Dictionaries an' all that. I bet if we talked about it for years an' years no one'd take any notice of us. They never do. They don' seem to want to have things jolly. Jus' fancy! Lent six weeks an' Christmas only one day. There isn't any *sense* in it."

"I bet they used to have a jollier time than we do at Christmas in the ole days," said Ginger. "You're always hearin' what fun people had at Christmas in the ole days."

"What did they do?" said William with interest.

"Oh, they had boars' heads an' waits an'——"

"Well, I bet I wouldn't like boars' heads—all teeth an' whatnot—an' we've tried bein' waits an' it didn't come off prop'ly. What else did they do in the ole days?"

"They did mumming," said Henry uncertainly.

"Mumming? What's mumming?" said William.

"It's sort of actin'," said Henry, still more uncertainly. "They were called mummers an' they—well, they did sort of actin'."

"Well, we've done that," said William. "We've done actin' but it always went wrong, somehow."

"But mumming wasn't ordin'ny actin'," said Henry.

"What sort was it, then?"

"I dunno, but I can find out," said Henry. "My father was talkin' about it last night."

"I bet it'll be somethin' silly," said William.

The others had forgotten the subject by the next day, but Henry turned up at the old barn full of importance.

"I've found out all about mummers," he said. "They jus' dressed up an' went dancin' about into people's houses an' people gave 'em money."

The Outlaws pricked up their ears.

"Gave 'em money?" said William. "Jus' for dancin' about?"

"Yes," said Henry. "One of 'em had to be St. George an' another the dragon, an' the rest jus' anyone an' they danced about an' people gave 'em money."

"It sounds easy," said William slowly. "I don't see why we shun't start that again. It'd be fun anyway an' we might get a bit of money. D'you say there's *got* to be St. George an' the dragon?"

"Yes, there's gotter be them."

"Well, St. George is all right," said William thoughtfully. "I mean, we can fix up him with saucepans an' things—but the dragon's goin' to be a bit of a bother."

"I say!" said Ginger excitedly. "I've jus' remembered. Freddie Parker's got a dragon suit. He's goin' to wear it at the Morrows' fancy-dress party next week, an' he's away this week. He's gone to stay with an aunt. He'd never know if we borrowed it. I bet Frankie would get it for us. He'd do anythin' for a bit of coconut ice."

They thought of Frankie Parker, Freddie's younger brother, a small snub-nosed freckled boy with a perverted craving for coconut ice.

"How much money have we got?" said William.

They discovered that they had twopence—enough, and more than enough, for their purpose.

"Come on," said William. "Let's go'n' find him now."

Frankie Parker was not hard to find. He was standing outside the village sweetshop, his nose flattened against the window, his eyes glued to a sticky mass of coconut ice that reposed on a soup plate inside.

"Hallo, Frankie," said William in a conciliatory tone.

"Hallo," said Frankie, without moving his eyes from the coconut ice.

"Like a bit of coconut ice?" went on William.

Frankie wheeled round eagerly.

"Yep," he said.

"Well, you've gotter earn it," said William.

"A' right," said Frankie. "What'll I do?"

"You know that dragon suit of Freddie's—the one he's goin' to wear at the Morrows'?"

"Uh-huh," agreed Frankie.

"Well, we jus' want to borrow it jus' for to-morrow. We'll take care of it an' Freddie'll never know."

Frankie looked rather thoughtful.

"I'll get in an awful row if he finds out," he said.

"We'll give you two pen'oth of coconut ice," said William.

Frankie's eyes gleamed. After all, two pen'oth of coconut ice was worth anything—even Freddie's vengeance.

"When'll you give it me?" he asked.

"A pen'oth now an' another pen'oth when you've got us the dragon suit," said William firmly.

"A' right," said Frankie. "Come on."

He entered the shop, followed by the Outlaws, and the owner, seeing Frankie, at once took the soup plate of coconut ice out of the window in readiness for his demands. He picked out the largest bar (Frankie was a good customer), William put the penny on the counter, and they all went out.

"You can have the other when you've got the dragon suit," said William firmly. "An' you needn't worry 'cause we'll take care of it all right."

Frankie certainly wasn't worrying. He was nibbling ecstatically at the large pink oblong of ambrosia that fate had so kindly and unexpectedly put in his way.

"You'll bring it after lunch, won't you?" said William anxiously.

Frankie made a sound of agreement through a mouthful of coconut ice and set off homeward.

He appeared duly at the old barn in the afternoon, carrying a paper parcel under his arm.

"There it is," he said, "an' I'll get in an awful row if Freddie finds out."

"He won't," William assured him. "Here's your coconut ice."

Frankie seized his guerdon eagerly and went off, nibbling. He turned round on a sudden thought. "I'll get you his Red Indian suit for two more," he said hopefully.

"We don't want his Red Indian suit," said William. "We've got one."

He was beginning to regret the second pen'oth. Frankie would probably have given them the whole of Freddie's wardrobe for one bar, or even half.

They watched the small squat figure disappear into the distance.

"He's beginning to look jus' like a piece of coconut ice himself," said Ginger dispassionately. "I bet his inside's nothing but it."

"Well, about the mummer stuff," said William. "We'll get it all fixed up to-day an' start it to-morrow. That'll be three days before Christmas. I bet we oughter make a jolly lot of money."

The dragon's costume turned out to be unexpectedly magnificent. There was a large head, with a mouth that showed gleaming white teeth, and a suit, with arms and legs made of some iridescent green material. It even had a tail—long and green and spiked at the end. They decided that William should wear the dragon suit and that Ginger—in the character of St. George—should wear a saucepan for a helmet, and a shield and breast-plate of cardboard and string that had originally been made by Robert for a charade. (Robert often vaguely wondered what had happened to it after the charade.) Douglas was to wear the Red Indian costume and Henry a paper crown and a dressing gown—a vague costume that might represent anything.

"We'll jus' go into each house an' dance about, same as you said," said William, and added doubtfully: "I hope it'll be all right."

* * *

They assembled in the early afternoon at the end of the village. The affair began all right, as affairs so often do. They visited Miss Milton, and she was delighted, inviting them into her little dining-room and letting them dance round and round her table. She even took the biscuit-barrel from the sideboard and handed it round. Her generosity, however, stopped short at that, and the Outlaws' delicacy forbade their suggesting any more satisfactory remuneration. The biscuits, moreover, were very plain and very dry and she only passed the barrel round once. Still, they were encouraged by the fact that she had obviously enjoyed the performance ("Delight-ful, dear children, quite delightful"), and that other people might enjoy it also and express their enjoyment in more lasting terms.

The next few visits were less satisfactory. Mrs. Burwash's maid gave them a glacial stare and slammed the door in their faces, muttering "You and your non-sense," as she did so. Mrs. Luton's maid did the same, and General Moult himself came to the door and shook his fist at them. They began to feel discouraged.

"Tell you what," said William. "I'll go into the nex'
one alone first an' explain about it. P'r'aps with us all
goin' in together an' startin' right away, they've sort of
not had time to take it in. I'll go'n' explain about us bein'
mummers an' tell 'em people used to give 'em money
an' all that an' then p'r'aps it'll be all right. You wait at
the gate while I go in an' tell 'em."

He walked up the short drive of the next house and
knocked at the front door. A girl of about ten came to it.
For a moment she appeared surprised to see the shining
green figure on the doorstep, then a look of concern
came into her face and she called: "Mother, here's
Freddie Parker. He's mistaken the day of the party.
What shall I do?"

Mrs. Morrow, stout and good-natured, bustled into
the hall. "Poor boy!" she said. "What a shame! Yes, his
mother was telling me about that costume. It's a lovely
one, isn't it? Well, of course, he must come in and stay to
tea. Come in, Freddie dear."

She held the door wide open and William, not knowing what else to do, entered. She patted his head reassuringly as he did so. "Poor boy!" she said again. "It *is* a
shame. It was *next* Tuesday, Freddie, not this. You must
have got the dates muddled."

William tried to open his mouth to explain matters to
her. He meant to pass very lightly over the dragon suit,
implying that it had been lent to him (as, of course, in a
way, it had) and concentrate on the mummer part of it
and especially the fact that mummers in the good old
days received pecuniary remuneration for their efforts.
But a terrible thing had happened. The stout lady's
reassuring pat had wedged the dragon head so firmly
over his head that his mouth wouldn't open. He put up

WILLIAM TRIED TO OPEN HIS MOUTH TO EXPLAIN MATTERS, BUT THE
DRAGON'S HEAD WAS WEDGED SO FIRMLY OVER HIS FACE THAT HIS
MOUTH WOULDN'T OPEN.

his hands to move it, but found it immovable. He could breathe—just breathe—but he couldn't speak or move the head. He tried again—again without success. The stout lady and the girl didn't seem to notice anything. They talked so much themselves that they never knew whether other people talked or not.

"You needn't take it off unless you want to, Freddie," said the stout lady. "It looks so nice. Come right in, dear. And never mind about it not being the day of the party. You shall stay to tea and have some nice games with Girlie and, of course, come again next Tuesday as well, and so you'll have two parties, won't you, dear? It doesn't really matter a bit, because Girlie here was just feeling bored and wanting someone to play with, weren't you, darling?"

William felt himself pushed into a room and seated at a table on which was a halma board.

"I was playing against myself," said Girlie, "but now, of course, I can play against you. You be green and I'll be red. Go on. You can start. Hurry up."

She had a shrill voice and a bossy manner. William had always disliked and avoided her. He'd never thought that he'd ever be sitting at a table playing halma with her . . . He hated the game, anyway. He played absently, racking his brains for some means of escape. He couldn't even make a sign to the others through the window, because this room was at the back of the house. He couldn't make any excuse to go because he couldn't speak. He couldn't just go because that would arouse their suspicions immediately. He was supposed to be Freddie Parker, who'd arrived on the wrong day for a party and presumably had all the afternoon at his disposal. Girlie kept up a continual stream of criticism. "Well, *aren't* you silly! Fancy moving it there. Mother,

Freddie *is* silly. Look, he's moved it so I can take six of his men. Wasn't it a *silly* thing to do?"

Mrs. Morrow sat by the open window, sewing and murmuring "Dear, dear!" "Well, well, well," as a sort of accompaniment to Girlie's shrill chatter.

Some caller arrived and was taken into the next room by Mrs. Morrow.

"Freddie Parker's here," William heard her saying. "The poor boy's mistaken the day of our party and come in his fancy dress. We're letting him stay to tea, of course, and he's having a lovely time playing with Girlie, so really the little monkey will have got two parties out of it."

"Oh, yes, I heard Freddie was back," said the visitor.

A horrible anxiety invaded William's soul. It was terrible to think that he was here walking abroad in Freddie's precious costume if it was true that Freddie was back. He was beginning to wish that he'd never heard of the wretched mummers or Freddie Parker or coconut ice. The caller went and Mrs. Morrow returned to the room.

The clock struck five.

"Tea-time!" she said brightly. "Now you'll have to take your head off—won't you, Freddie?—or you won't be able to eat any tea."

William was just wondering whether to make a dash for liberty when there came a ring at the front door and Girlie went to open it. A shrill scream came from the hall.

"Freddie *Parker*! . . . But it *can't* be. He's here already."

Then Freddie's voice was heard in the hall, explaining volubly that he'd come home because a friend of his cousin's had got scarlet fever and the cousin had to go into quarantine, but it would be all right about the party—wouldn't it?—because he'd never actually met the friend and——

He realised at last that Girlie and her mother (who had now joined Girlie at the front door) were staring at him with expressions of helpless amazement on their faces, and then, suddenly, through the open doorway, he caught sight of William struggling in a last frantic effort to free his head before making a dash for liberty. Freddie uttered a howl of rage. His costume. His treasured costume. The costume that on Tuesday was to blaze suddenly upon an astonished world and put every other costume in the neighbourhood to shame . . . parading itself here publicly without his knowledge or consent. He sprang forward furiously. William, abandoning the attempt to free his head, leapt instinctively for the nearest exit, which happened to be the open window. Freddie, all other considerations lost in a flaming sense of grievance, pushed Girlie and her mother aside and leapt after him. The two vanished from sight, leaving Mrs. Morrow and Girlie clinging to each other in dismay.

"How can there be two of him, mother?" demanded Girlie.

"I don't know, dear," said Mrs. Morrow, faintly.

William was the fleeter of the two, but his sight was somewhat impeded, so that it was all he could do to keep ahead of his pursuer. He climbed over the back gate of Mrs. Morrow's garden and plunged into the narrow lane that ran behind it. Freddie followed close on his heels. Through a hole in the hedge and across a field . . . Over a gate and back along another lane . . . Down the main road, only a yard or two in front of Freddie . . . William sprinted suddenly ahead, rounded a corner and dodged in at a pair of big gates, hoping that Freddie would go straight on down the road, but Freddie didn't. He came in at the gates, too. William fled up the drive, Freddie behind him, coming nearer and nearer. There was an open French window at the end of the drive. It somehow suggested a refuge, and William plunged into it. . . .

* * *

The Outlaws waited for William at the gate of Mrs. Morrow's house—at first expectantly, then growing more and more bewildered as the moments passed, and he did not reappear.

Ginger cautiously approached the house and looked in at the front windows, but no one and nothing was to be seen.

"I say, what'd we better do?" he said, returning to the others. " 'S no good jus' stayin' here."

"Let's go on an' do a bit of mummin'," suggested Douglas. "We might get some money. Then we'll come back an' see if he's come out yet. If we waste any more time the afternoon'll be over an' we won't've done any mummin' at all."

This seemed a sensible suggestion. Certainly it wasn't any use just standing at the gate any longer.

"He's sure to find us when he comes out," said Henry. "P'r'aps they only wanted one mummer here. Anyway, I bet he'd want us to get on with it. Come on."

They went down to the road and along the road, feeling desolate and leaderless and hoping that they were doing the right thing.

The first house they visited proved to be empty. At the next a deaf old man came to the door and told them he didn't want anything. The next looked rather imposing, and at first they hesitated about trying it.

"Come on," said Ginger at last. "They c'n only send us away, an' p'r'aps they'll like it an' give us somethin'. It's got a rich sort of door, anyway."

They walked up to the door—tall and massive and six-panelled. Ginger rang the bell. A maid opened it, and at once a harassed-looking middle-aged woman came into the hall.

"Who is it?" she asked.

"We're mummers," said Ginger, speaking rather timidly and wishing that William were there to deal with the situation. "Can we come in an'—an' mum for you?"

"I never heard such nonsense," said the woman indignantly. "Go away at once."

Just then another woman, rather like the first one but more harassed-looking, joined them.

"What is it, dear?" she asked.

"They say they're mummers," said the first lady. "I never heard such nonsense. I've told them to go away at once. Really, it's too much—on the top of father being so difficult to-day."

"Oh, *but*," said the other eagerly, putting out an arm to detain the mummers, "he's just been talking about mummers. He remembers them when he was a boy. He says that he and his friends used to play at being mummers at Christmas. It might interest him and put him in a better temper. One never knows . . ."

The other looked uncertain.

"Very well," she said at last. "I don't think it will, but anything's worth trying. I've never *known* him so cantankerous as he is to-day. Come in, then, boys, and wipe your feet."

The three Outlaws entered somewhat sheepishly.

They had a horrible suspicion that without William the whole thing would fall flat.

"This way," said the first woman, throwing open a door.

They entered a large room. An old man sat in a chair by the fireplace, his knees wrapped in a rug. He looked the most bad-tempered old man the Outlaws had ever seen. He had a thin grim line of a mouth and long white side-whiskers. His deep-set eyes glared fiercely behind straggling white eyebrows.

"Who are these?" he said angrily.

"They're mummers, father," said one of the women timidly. "Boys playing at mummers. You remember you said you used to when you were a boy. I thought perhaps . . ."

The old man looked the Outlaws up and down disparagingly.

"Don't look like mummers to me," he said. "No St. George or dragon."

Ginger opened his mouth to explain that he was St. George and they were going to imagine the dragon, but the old man silenced him with a growl. "Red Indian costumes and dressing-gowns. No sense in it. We'd got more gumption in my day. You should have seen our dragon. Well, get on with it. Get on with it. Get on with it."

The three Outlaws began to dance about the room uncertainly, apprehensively. They were regretting having come at all. They might have known it wouldn't be any good without William. They weren't surprised to see the old man growing angrier every moment.

"Rubbishy performance!" he stormed. "Rubbishy, I tell you! Rubbishy! Get out, all of you. How you have the impudence to come here and pretend . . ." He almost choked with rage.

"GO ON, ALL OF YOU," CRIED THE OLD MAN. "IT'S A RUBBISHY
PERFORMANCE!"

THEN A DRAGON RUSHED IN THROUGH THE WINDOW, CLOSELY PURSUED BY A BOY.

"I *told* you so," wailed the woman who'd opened the door.

"Get away with you!" roared the old man, reaching for his stick.

The Outlaws were turning to flee before him when an unexpected thing happened. In at the French window rushed a dragon, closely pursued by a boy.

The dragon tried to get under the table, but the boy was upon him at once, and the two of them began to struggle fiercely on the floor in the middle of the room. Sometimes the dragon was on top, sometimes the boy. They snarled and wrestled and punched and kicked. The old man clapped his hands, laughing delightedly.

"Excellent! Excellent!" he cried. "I didn't know you'd got that up your sleeve. Most effective! Capital performance! Congratulate you both!"

Freddie Parker sat up and gaped at him. He wanted to explain his intrusion and describe the dastardly trick that William had played on him, but he hadn't any breath. Running and fighting had taken it all away. The struggle had loosened the dragon's head and William now took it off, revealing a purple, perspiring face. The old man was still clapping heartily, so were the two women, so were Ginger and Henry and Douglas. Freddie's look of fury changed to one of bewilderment.

"Splendid! Splendid!" the old man was saying. "St. George should have worn some sort of armour, of course, but it would probably have come off, so perhaps it was more sensible not to attempt it. Coming in at the window like that was a capital idea."

He dived into a pocket and, taking out a wallet, drew from it a pound note which he handed to William.

"Divide that between your company," he said, "with my heartiest congratulations."

"Thanks very much," said William. "That'll be four shillings each. I say, that's jolly good of you."

"Not at all, not at all," said the old man. "I thoroughly enjoyed it."

"I *told* you so," said the second woman.

Freddie Parker opened and shut his mouth. He didn't understand what had happened, but he realised that this was no time for explanations. Moreover, he definitely gathered that four shillings were to fall to his lot.

Explanations could—and would—come later, but already something of his animosity towards William was fading. They'd had a good fight, and it's an expensive hatchet that can't be buried for four shillings. . . .

Chapter 6

William Starts the New Year

"It's New Year's Day to-morrow," said Ginger.

"Yes, I know," said William gloomily. "My mother was talkin' about it an' sayin' we oughter make good resolutions about bein' tidy an' punctual an' clean an' suchlike."

"So was mine," said Ginger.

"Well, I think it's silly," said William heatedly, "wastin' a lot of time over little things like bein' tidy an' punctual an' clean. I'd rather do somethin' big."

"What?" asked Ginger with interest.

"I've not thought it out yet," admitted William. "But if I start the New Year, same as what they say, I'll not do it by silly little things like bein' tidy an' punctual an' clean. I'll do it by somethin' that'll make me famous."

"You couldn't," said Ginger with conviction. "Not in one day."

"How d'you know I couldn't?" retorted William. "I've done lots of things in one day that people never thought I could. Anyway, I could start it. I'm sick of goin' on an' on an' on an' doin' nothin' to make me famous. Why, it's a whole year since—since—well, since this time las' year an' I'm no nearer bein' famous than I was then. I've tried all sorts of things—explorin' an' bein' a detective an' gettin' up shows—an' none of 'em have ever made me famous. I've gotter start soon or it'll be too late.''

Ginger saw that William was in one of his rare moods of depression and set about cheering him.

"People don't gen'rally get famous till they've grown up," he said reassuringly.

"No, but I bet they start practisin' bein' famous long before that," said William. "I bet explorers start practisin' explorin' an' detectives detectin' an' dictators dictatin' long before they're grown up. Stands to reason they do. Well, I've tried nearly everythin', an' it's always turned out wrong. It wasn't my fault any of the times, but no one would believe it wasn't."

"Well, never mind," said Ginger. "I bet somethin'll turn up soon."

"I've thought of money-lendin', but I never have any money to lend and no one ever pays me back when I do. 'Sides, money-lenders aren't reely famous—not the way I want to be. Then I've thought of leadin' a rebellion, only there aren't any rebellions nowadays. I bet it's much harder to get famous now than it was in hist'ry. Well, anyway," he brightened, "it's nearly tea-time an' I'm goin' home. Cook was makin' gingerbreads this mornin' an' I don't want to miss 'em . . .''

He hurried homewards, his spirits rising. Cook's gingerbreads were specially delicious, and he felt that he might leave his future fame to fate for the time being and concentrate his whole attention upon them.

It was not quite tea-time when William reached home, but he found a neighbour, Miss Milton, in the drawing-room having tea with his mother. She was holding forth very earnestly and with much gesticulation, and Mrs. Brown was looking somewhat bewildered. Miss Milton turned to William, greeted him absently, then continued:

"You see, Mrs. Brown," she said, "I want it to be a great social movement sweeping the whole of England. It will solve, I am sure, all our social problems. I want every family of ordinary means to adopt a poor family— to give them cast-off clothing, plants from the garden, food, financial assistance and—er—to help solve all their little problems for them."

"But we *couldn't*," gasped Mrs. Brown.

Miss Milton waved aside her objections.

"I am starting it first of all in this village. Every upper or middle class family will, I hope, adopt a poor family, and I am sure that the Movement will soon spread all over England. Just think of it. Every poor family under the protection of a well-to-do one. There will be no more poverty. There will be no more class warfare. There will be no more communism or fascism or—or anything. We will be a large happy contented family—all helping each other and—well, all helping each other. It will spread all over the world. It will bring the millennium in its train."

"But, Miss Milton——" began Mrs. Brown.

Miss Milton again waved aside the interruption.

"I have here," she went on, taking a piece of paper from her pocket, "a list of the poor families in this district and I want you to select one. I suggest that, as you have young people in your family, you choose one with young people. Here is one with six girls and three boys. Your young people could help these young people in many ways. They could have them to tea, try to interest them in the arts, take them away on camping holidays in the summer——"

"Miss Milton," said Mrs. Brown, so firmly that Miss Milton actually stopped talking to listen to her, "I'm sorry, but I can't even *consider* the idea. It's all my husband can do to support his own family, and——"

"But even if you can't help financially," persisted Miss Milton, "you can surely give them food and cast-off clothes and plants from the garden and that sort of thing."

"I can't," said Mrs. Brown firmly. "I don't want to. I think it's a dreadful idea. I'm sorry to say it, but I really do."

Miss Milton rose in majestic displeasure.

"I'm sorry that that is your attitude, Mrs. Brown. I won't waste any more of your time, then . . . Good afternoon."

She swept out haughtily, ignoring William and knocking over a small cake-stand that stood by the door.

Mrs. Brown heaved a deep sigh, partly of exasperation and partly of relief.

"I never *heard* such nonsense," she said. "Now, William, go upstairs and wash your hands and tidy your hair. It's nearly your tea-time."

William went slowly upstairs. He had been deeply impressed by the visitor's harangue, and he strongly disapproved of his mother's attitude. If the results that Miss Milton had prophesied would really follow from the scheme (and William, ever an optimist, didn't see why they shouldn't), then he thought it very wrong and foolish of his mother to dismiss it so unceremoniously. He ate his tea absent-mindedly, but not so absent-mindedly as not to do full justice to the plate of gingerbreads.

"*William!*" said Mrs. Brown, coming in as he was just finishing the last one. "You've not eaten *all* those gingerbreads!"

William looked at the empty plate as if seeing it for the first time.

"I 'spect I have," he said. He spoke rather regretfully, for his mind had been so taken up by Miss Milton's plan that he felt he really hadn't savoured to its utmost the deliciousness of the vanished dainties. "Can't I have any more?"

"Of course not, William. You must have eaten *dozens*."

"They're jolly thin," said William. "It takes nearly a dozen of them to make a proper mouthful. I say, mother"—he carefully collected all the crumbs from the gingerbread plate and put them in his mouth—" I think that thing Miss Milton was talking about was a jolly good idea."

"It was ridiculous, William," said Mrs. Brown with spirit.

"Well, if it'd stop all poverty, same as what she said, an' all communism an' suchlike an' spread all over the world, I think it's jolly good. I think you oughter join in with it. It might make us all famous."

"Don't be absurd, William," said Mrs. Brown. "Anyway, I've simply no time for things like that."

William had in justice to allow that this was true. His mother was occupied in household tasks from morning to night, and one really couldn't expect her to adopt a poor family as well. But there was no reason why he, William, shouldn't. He had plenty of time before term began, and, as a matter of fact, he had been secretly feeling a little bored since Christmas. He couldn't adopt a whole family, of course, but he could adopt the children or one of the children. He could take them plants from the garden and bits of food and some of his clothes. It would be a good start to the new year anyway. It mightn't make him famous, of course, but on the other hand it might. One never knew. And it would

e interesting. He considered whether to take up the
cheme jointly with the other Outlaws, but resolved,
inally, to try it out on his own, and, if it was successful,
o bring in the others and organise it on a large scale.
Yes—his spirits rose at the thought—it might quite well
make him famous.

In order to waste no further time he quickly collected
he crumbs that were left on the bread and butter plate,
wallowed them with two spoonfuls of jam, put the
mpty milk-jug on the tea pot spout to amuse the
ousemaid when she came to clear away, then went out
nto the garden to start operations. Miss Milton had
een very emphatic about plants, so William pulled up
everal wintry-looking roots and stuffed them into his
ocket. Then he stood, considering . . . Food . . , he
must take some food. She'd been emphatic about food,
oo. Pity they'd been so stingy with the gingerbreads or
e might have taken some of them. After all, even Miss
Milton couldn't expect him to starve himself for the
oor. He walked slowly round to the larder window and,
inding it ajar, opened it cautiously. There was a dish of
am turnovers near, and William, stretching out his arm
o its utmost, could just reach one of them. He stuffed it
nto his pocket among the roots and beat a hasty retreat.
Then he stood in the front garden again, considering the
osition. Clothes? Miss Milton had said something
bout clothes. Well, he'd got a lot of clothes he didn't
want—only his mother would probably make an awful
uss when she found he'd taken them. Besides, it would
e difficult to get them out of the house without her
nowledge. She always seemed to appear in the hall
whenever he was coming downstairs with anything he
articularly didn't want her to see. It would have to be
omething small. An idea occurred to him. His gloves.

An aunt had given him a pair of brown leather gloves fo
Christmas and his mother was always making him wea
them. He'd give his gloves to his poor family. It was
splendid idea. He felt a glow of virtue and exhilaratior
He'd be doing a good deed and getting rid of the beastl
things. His mother came into the hall as he was comin
downstairs.

"What are you doing with your gloves, dear?" sh
said.

"Oh, I thought I might as well wear 'em," sai
William airily. " 'Cause—'cause of bein' tidy same a
what you're always sayin'."

"But you musn't wear those, William. Your ol
woollen ones are somewhere about. I'm glad you'r
beginning to take a pride in your appearance, dear, bu
you must keep these beautiful gloves that Auntie Flossi
gave you for best."

Her gaze travelled to his pocket, and a look of con
sternation came into her face. Seeing it, William hastil
made his way out of the front door, putting the gloves o
the hat-stand as he passed.

"*William!*" called Mrs. Brown. "What have you go
in your pocket?"

William, who had now reached the front gate, walke
into the road, apparently without hearing, then hurrie
off in the direction of Hadley. He had decided tha
Hadley should be the scene of his operations. In Hadle
there were many mean narrow streets behind the mai
road, where poor people lived, and he ought to fin
there some suitable candidate for adoption. Money
Miss Milton had mentioned money. He had a penny i
his pocket underneath the roots and jam turnover. Tha
would have to do for the present. He'd have some mor
on Saturday when he got his pocket money. At least, h

oped he would. He would if no one had discovered the rack in the back window of the tool-shed where his ball ad just touched it by accident the day before yesterday. t was a pity about the gloves. He'd have to give omething he'd got on. His handkerchief, perhaps. That would be better than nothing. It was all right about the ood and the plants, anyway. He patted his pocket omplacently, blending its contents still further together.

Having reached Hadley, he strolled uncertainly along he main street for some way then went down a side urning that led to a row of small cottages. He meant to be more careful than he had been on the occasion when he'd looked for a poor family in order to relieve them of heir dog. He must find a small one and one preferably without a father. He walked past the cottages, round a corner, into another long narrow street . . . then stopped abruptly. A little girl was leaning against the wall, eating a toffee-apple on a stick. She was nibbling round it in a circle, her whole attention absorbed by the process. William looked at her. Beneath its covering of grime, her face was distinctly pretty. Fair curly hair hung about t in picturesque disorder. She wore a faded red coat, with a collar of moth-eaten fur, buttoned tight up to the neck. The grubby little hand that held the toffee-apple was adorned with two rings and a bracelet. William's heart leapt in sudden admiration.

"Hallo," he said ingratiatingly.

She looked at him, her teeth still embedded in the toffee-apple, then contracted the upper part of her face in a grimace indicative of dislike and contempt and went on nibbling. William's admiration increased.

"D'you want a penny?" he said.

The little girl finished her toffee-apple in two large

business-like bites and threw the stick into the gutter.

"Oo's got one?" she demanded.

"I have," said William. "I'll buy you another toffee apple if you like."

"A' right," said the little girl. " 'E's jus' roun there."

She led him round another corner, where an old ma slowly wheeled a little cart of toffee-apples, crying hi wares in a thin ghostlike voice.

"They're ha'penny each," said the little girl "Where's your penny?"

William burrowed in a pocket, bringing out bits of soi and root and jam turnover inextricably intermingled.

"What's that?" said the little girl with interest.

"It—it was a sort of present for you," said William who had by now decided that the little girl would suitabl fulfil the role of adoptee. "Plants for your garden an suchlike."

"I ain't got no garding an' I don't want no mess plants," said the little girl indignantly. "I never seed n plants neither with bits of jam an' plumstones all ove 'em like that."

"Oh, that," said William carelessly. "That was a sor of tart I was bringing you. It's sort of got squashed up that's all." He inspected the mixture anxiously. "Yo can pick the tart out easy. There's quite a lot stuck on th roots. Look! That's a jolly big piece."

The little girl took the piece he was pointing to and pu it in her mouth, then spat it violently out on to th pavement.

"Nothin' but stones an' dirt!" she said indignantly "An' if you're tryin' to be funny with me——"

"No, I'm not," William hastened to assure her "Honest, I'm not. I thought that bit was all right. Well 'll throw it all away then." He threw the mixture, egretfully, into the gutter. "I took a jolly lot of trouble over it. It's a jolly good jam tart an' I bet that plant's a olly good one, too. I bet they'll make enough fuss about t, anyway, when they find it's gone, whether it's a good one or not."

He burrowed farther into his pocket and finally prought out a coin, its face obliterated by jam and soil. He wiped it clean on his trousers.

"There you are!" he said triumphantly. "There's the penny. Told you I'd got one. Now come on. Let's get the coffee-apple."

They ran up to the old man, bought two halfpenny coffee-apples, and walked down the street side by side, nibbling happily.

"What's your name?" said William.

"Gert," said the little girl. "What's yours?"

"William. Where do you live?"

"There," said Gert, pointing to one of the small houses that lined the street. William considered the house carefully. Yes, despite her personal charm, Gert obviously belonged to the class so sweepingly designated by Miss Milton as the Poor, and William felt relieved at having solved his problem so quickly and so happily. He was just about to explain the position to his protégé when she suddenly said:

"Nah, where's that bloomin' kid?"

"What bloomin' kid?" said William.

"Our Albert. I'm jus' about *sick* of 'im. Never get a minute's peace with 'im, I don't."

"Why not?" said William interested.

"Always gotter be a-mindin' of 'im or a-washin' of 'im or a-dressin' of 'im," said Gert bitterly. "Can't do nothink nor go nowheres for 'im. Don't matter what I

want to do, I can't never do it. Can't never go to the
pictures 'cept when 'e's in bed. 'No, you stay round an'
mind Albert,' says Ma. *Sick* of 'im, I am, an' no mistake!
Al-*bert!*"

The cry, which would have put a factory siren to
shame, shattered even William's hardy nerves for a
second. He blenched as she repeated it.

"LOOK AT 'IM," SAID GERT. "CAN'T KEEP CLEAN FOR TWO
MINUTES, 'E CAN'T."

"Al-*bert!*"

The second summons had its effect. A small boy of about five, wearing a baggy suit much too large for him and a man's tweed cap pulled low down over his eyes, came lounging round the corner.

"Look at 'im," said Gert dispassionately. "Can't keep clean for two minutes, 'e can't. Even Ma sez 'e's a trile. 'A proper trile, 'e is, an' no mistake,' she sez."

"Does your father like him?" said William, at the back of whose mind a vague plan was stirring.

"Dad don't 'ardly ever see 'im," said Gert. " 'E's in bed when Dad goes to work in the mornin' an' 'e's in bed again when 'e comes 'ome. Only time we any of us get any peace, when 'e's in bed. Ma says she's fair wore out with 'im sometimes, and I can tell you I am. Can't never go nowheres nor do nothink for 'im. It's sickenin'. Come on, Albert. Time you was in bed."

Albert, however, was evidently not ready for bed. He doubled suddenly down the street from which he had come and only after a long interval was finally captured and brought back, struggling and kicking and howling, by a red-faced Gert. He was finally dragged inside the house that Gert had pointed to and the door shut.

William stood gazing at the front door. He remembered suddenly that he hadn't given her the handkerchief and, taking it out of his pocket, examined it, wondering whether to knock at the door and present it. It was sodden with jam and damp soil and indeed suggested a greasing-rag more than an article of toilet. Reluctantly he restored it to his pocket. Perhaps she wouldn't like it. Girls, he knew, were funny about such things. And, anyway, he'd fulfilled most of the other conditions. He'd given her food and money. Miss Milton, however, had said that adopters must help to

solve the little problems of the adoptees. That was what
he must now turn his mind to. And Gert's little problem
was obviously Albert.

He went home and ate his supper absently, still
thinking of Albert. He went to bed absently, still thinking of Albert. He went to sleep, still thinking of Albert.
He dreamed that Albert, in his baggy suit with his cap
over his eyes, suddenly grew as large as an elephant and
pursued him through the back streets of Hadley, waving
a gigantic toffee-apple. He awoke and sat up in bed and
once more thought of Albert. Gert and her family must
be delivered from the bondage of Albert. Gert couldn't
do nothink nor go nowheres for him, her mother found
him a proper trile, and his father hardly ever saw him, so
wouldn't care either way. But what was to be done with
Albert? Where was he to be removed to? And then,
quite suddenly, an idea flashed into William's mind—so
simple that he wondered he hadn't thought of it before,
so comprehensive that it seemed to solve the whole
problem. Albert should be adopted by Miss Milton.
After all, the idea of adopting the poor had originated
from her, therefore it was only right that she should
relieve Gert of Albert, with his kickings and screamings
and baggy suit. There was ample room in Miss Milton's
house for him and he was sure that, once she realised the
situation, she would acquiesce with delight. Having
solved the problem to his complete satisfaction, William
lay down again and went to sleep. When he awoke in the
morning, the solution—as generally happens in such
cases—seemed less simple in its details than it had
seemed in the night, but still it remained the only
possible one. Gert must be freed from Albert, and Miss
Milton, with her wholesale ideas on adoption, would
surely take a little thing like Albert in her stride.

He meant to go in search of Albert in the morning, but his mother insisted on his accompanying her to buy a new pair of shoes. She said that she didn't know what he did with his shoes, and William replied that he only walked on them same as other people and that he couldn't help his things wearing out natural, same as everyone else's did. He wasn't a ghost. He supposed that ghosts never wore their shoes out, but he couldn't help not being a ghost, could he? As a matter of fact he'd rather like to be a ghost. He thought they must have a lot of fun, scaring people out of their lives at Christmas an' suchlike. Mrs. Brown brought the conversation back to shoes and said it was crawling on the tops of walls and climbing trees and dragging the toes in the dust that ruined them, not ordinary wear, and William said why didn't she get him a pair of iron shoes then? He'd rather like a pair of iron shoes. Same as knights wore with their suits of armour goin' into battle.

He'd like a suit of armour, too. He'd always wanted one. He couldn't understand why people had stopped wearing them. They must be much more fun than ordinary clothes. They—but they'd reached the shoe shop now, and the business of buying the shoes began. Mrs. Brown chose finally a very stout pair with apparently impenetrable toecaps. William regarded them with disfavour and held forth once more on the advantage of suits of armour as compared with modern clothing. Mrs. Brown told him to stop talking such nonsense for goodness' sake, and took him with her to the grocer's, baker's and coal merchant's, and when they'd finished this it was time for lunch. William decided to go in search of Albert immediately afterwards. He was anxious to get the business settled.

As soon as lunch was over he slipped quietly out of the

house and made his way down to Hadley to the stree
where he'd met Gert. Gert, however, rather to hi
disappointment, was nowhere to be seen. He'd hav
liked to dally a little with Gert before starting the seriou
business of Albert's adoption. Moreover, his mothe
had given him a penny for going with her to get the nev
shoes in the morning, and he had spent this on tw
toffee-apples, which he meant to present to Gert. Sud
denly, as he was gazing nonplussed up and down th
empty street, the small and baggy figure of Alber
appeared at the corner. That recalled William to hi
immediate duty. He approached Albert and held out t
him one of the toffee-apples. Albert took it and began t
nibble at it appreciatively.

"Come on," said William, showing him the other
"You've gotter come with me. You can have this whei
we've got to where we're goin'."

He took Albert's hand, and Albert, still nibbling, se
off with him trustingly. Having arrived at the village
William made his way towards Miss Milton's house, stil
holding the trusting Albert by the hand. It occurred t
him suddenly and for the first time that perhaps Mis
Milton should have been consulted, but he reassurec
himself by the reflection that her consent could surely b
taken for granted. After all, hadn't she inspired th
whole proceeding? Wasn't she prepared to adopt th
entire body of the Poor of England? What, then, was a
little thing like Albert to her more or less? Havin
reached her house, William stood for a momen
uncertain, then, firmly grasping Albert by the hand, h
rang the bell. No one answered. He rang again. Still nc
one answered. He knocked. Still no one answered
Somewhat disconcerted, he went round to the back o
the house, followed by the docile Albert, now busil

engaged on the second toffee-apple. The kitchen door stood ajar. Miss Milton was out and her maid had taken the opportunity to go to the post, where she had met one of her admirers, a window-cleaner, who was keeping her—by no means against her will—engaged in conversation.

William had felt disconcerted only for a moment. For a sudden memory had occurred to him. He had been to the pictures just before Christmas to see a Silly Symphony and had had to sit through a sentimental film in which the life of a sad and lonely spinster had been made happy and busy by the adoption of a small boy. The boy—an orphan—had walked into the spinster's house of his own accord, got into her bed, and fallen asleep. The sad and lonely spinster had gone to her bedroom on her return and found the cherubic little head nestling on her pillow. She had leaned over it with clasped hands, and large tears (you could see them quite plainly) had dropped from her eyes on to the small sleeping cherub, surprisingly without waking him. The memory seemed to solve the immediate difficulty. Albert must be put into Miss Milton's bed—then she could come back and cry over him and devote the rest of her life to him, like the lady in the picture.

He led Albert upstairs to the front bedroom, which, he rightly concluded, was Miss Milton's. There he looked first at the bed, with its neat counterpane of Indian embroidery, and then at Albert.

"Now, Albert," he explained carefully, "you're goin' to live here. You're goin' to be Miss Milton's little boy. She's adopted you an' she'll look after you an' buy you everythin' you want."

Albert considered this prospect in silence. He seemed pleased and interested.

"Will she buy me toffee-apples?" he asked.

"Yes," said William.

"An' ice-cream cornets?"

"Yes," promised William.

"An' shrimps?"

"Yes," said William, to whom these all seemed reasonable enough requests.

"And let me stay up long as I like nights?"

"Yes," promised William, who was sure that Miss Milton, being notoriously absent-minded, would never notice what time Albert went to bed.

"An' gimme twopence Saturday 'stead of only a penny?"

"Yes, I'm sure she will," said William.

"A' right," said Albert, who now seemed quite reconciled to his change of parents and residence.

"Well, now all you've gotter do," said William briskly, "is to get into that bed an' stay there till she comes in. Then she'll cry over you an'—an' start buyin' you things straight away."

"Don't want ter go ter bed," objected Albert.

"You needn't go right to bed," said William. "Jus' get in an' pull the things over you an' wait till she comes in an' starts cryin' over you. You can get up after that."

Albert allowed himself to be helped into the neat little bed and the clothes pulled over him. There he lay, nibbling the remains of his toffee-apple, his cap still pulled down over his childish but highly unprepossessing face. William stood and looked at him doubtfully, remembering the dimpled cherubic countenance surrounded by the mass of sunny curls, that had so touched the heart of the spinster in the picture. Somehow, Albert didn't look a bit like that. He removed the large tweed cap, but Albert's hair, lank and untended, seemed such

WILLIAM LOOKED AT HIM DOUBTFULLY. ALBERT WAS PLACIDLY
NIBBLING HIS TOFFEE-APPLE.

a mean substitute for the mass of sunny curls that he put
t back again. After all, Miss Milton might prefer Albert
to the child in the picture. He'd thought himself that
the child in the picture was a bit soppy. Heartened
by this reflection, he gave final instructions to Albert to
shut his eyes when Miss Milton came in and not open
them till he felt her tears on his face, then went downstairs.

The kitchen door was still ajar, for Miss Milton's maid

was still dallying with the window-cleaner at the pillar-
box. (She'd already half promised to go to the pictures
with him to-morrow night.) William set off briskly down
the road to Hadley again. He must now find Gert and tell
her the good news. He was taking a jolly lot of trouble
over it, he assured himself complacently. Miss Milton
ought to be jolly grateful to him when she found out.

Meantime Albert remained in Miss Milton's bed till
he had finished what was left of his toffee-apple, then
turned his attention to the immediate future. He didn't
object to being adopted by Miss Milton (according to her
deputy, she had quite enlightened ideas on the upbring-
ing of children), but he didn't want to stay in bed on a
fine afternoon and be cried over. Deciding to cut out that
part of the programme, therefore, he rose and made his
way downstairs. The cap fell off as he got out of bed, and
he didn't stay to pick it up. The kitchen door was still
ajar, so Albert made his way cautiously out into the
road. He wandered along aimlessly, swaggering a little,
for he felt proud of his new status as an adopted boy, till
he reached the gate of the Vicarage. There he stood
looking in. It seemed an interesting garden, and he
didn't see why he shouldn't go in and explore. He felt
that now he'd been adopted the whole place more or less
belonged to him. He walked up the drive and was going
round the side of the house to the lawn at the back of it
when Mrs. Monks, the Vicar's wife, came out of a side
door.

"What do you want, little boy?" she said.

"Nothink," said Albert calmly, and went on walking
round to the back of the house.

Mrs. Monks, somewhat disconcerted, followed him.

"Er—what's your name?" she said.

"Albert," said Albert nonchalantly.

"What's your other name? I mean, whose little boy are you?"

"Miss Milton's," said Albert.

"Miss Milton's?" said the Vicar's wife in amazement. "But that's not true, Albert. I know that Miss Milton hasn't got any little boys."

"She's 'dopted me," said Albert importantly.

"What?" said the Vicar's wife, still more amazed.

"She's 'dopted me," repeated Albert.

There was something so convincing in his manner that Mrs. Monks went indoors and fetched her husband.

"This little boy says that Miss Milton's adopted him," she said.

"Well, then, my dear, I suppose she has," said the Vicar, who wasn't particularly interested in Miss Milton's affairs and wanted to get back to his sermon.

"Did she send you here?" said Mrs. Monks.

Albert wondered whether to say "yes" or "no" and decided finally on "yes" because it seemed simpler. Mrs. Monks looked at her husband.

"I suppose that's her way of telling us. I remember now she passed me on her bicycle in the village about half an hour ago and called out, 'I've got a surprise for you.' She must have meant this. How wonderful! What a difference it will make to her life!"

The Vicar looked at Albert without any marked enthusiasm.

"I'm sure it will," he said, and returned to his sermon.

"Come in, dear boy," said Mrs. Monks winningly to Albert. "Come in and tell me all about it."

Albert followed Mrs. Monks into the drawing-room. There Mrs. Monks looked him over a little doubtfully. Really, Miss Milton ought to turn the child out better than this. He was shockingly dirty and was dressed in very common and badly fitting clothes.

"When did Miss Milton adopt you, dear boy?" she said.

"This afternoon," said Albert.

That explained it, of course. Miss Milton was probably out now buying the child some decent clothes and she'd probably washed him quite recently. Children got dirty in a notoriously short space of time. It was rather odd of her to send the child in with the news like this, but then Miss Milton had always been rather odd. Perhaps the child would make her more normal. She had done a wonderful deed in adopting the child, of course, and one must help her all one could. Mrs. Monks led Albert to the bathroom and washed his hands and face. Albert submitted reluctantly but resignedly. One couldn't really hope to escape washing even by adoption. He'd suspected that from the first. Still, there were the ice-cream cornets and shrimps and toffee-apples that had been definitely promised him.

Mrs. Monks was leading him downstairs.

"Did Miss Milton say she was coming to fetch you after tea?" she asked.

"Yes," said Albert. He generally said "yes" except when the form of the question seemed to demand "no". He found it saved trouble.

"You must come and have some tea, then," said Mrs. Monks brightly.

Tea was laid in the drawing-room on a small low table at the fireside. Mrs. Monks looked doubtfully from her guest to the carpet. He was obviously the type of child who'd manage to spread crumbs for yards around him even if you sat him right up to the table. A bright idea occurred to her.

"It's quite a fine afternoon, dear," she said. "Wouldn't you like to take your tea out to the summer-house and have it there? Just for a little treat?" she added coaxingly.

"Yes," agreed Albert.

"And you can have this ball to play with," went on Mrs. Monks, taking from a drawer a ball that she had confiscated from a choir boy at choir practice the evening before.

She poured out a cup of tea, put some bread and butter and cake on a plate, gave the ball to Albert, took him down to the summer-house at the end of the lawn, and laid cup and plate on the table before him.

"There, dear!" she said brightly. "Isn't that nice? Now you can have a nice tea all by yourself, can't you?"

She lifted him on to the seat and escaped indoors, pleased by her little manœuvre. She disliked children at the best of times and found Albert a peculiarly unattractive specimen, which made it still more wonderful of Miss Milton to have adopted him, of course. The child of some relative, perhaps. He looked terribly common, but even Miss Milton might have common relatives. The very best people had . . . (At this moment Miss Milton's maid was gazing with rising consternation at the traces of recent occupation of Miss Milton's bed, the smears of toffee-apple on the pillow and the man's tweed cap that lay on the floor by the bedside.)

Mrs. Monks had almost finished her tea when Miss Milton arrived. Miss Milton had had rather a disappointing day. People had been strangely lukewarm about her wonderful scheme, and the reluctance of well-to-do families to adopt poor ones had been as nothing compared with the reluctance of poor families to be adopted. Indeed, Miss Milton, propounding her scheme in the

cottages of the neighbourhood, had been, on more than
one occasion, forcibly ejected. But she'd just had a
wonderful success. She'd been to see General Moult
who usually refused with unnecessary vehemence to
participate in any of her schemes, and much to her
surprise he'd said that she could put his name down on
her list. She could not know, of course, that General
Moult, who was very deaf, thought that she was asking
for a subscription to the Parish Magazine and said,
"Yes, yes, yes. You can put my name down on your
list," merely in order to get rid of her. He'd refused to
give her a subscription to the Parish Magazine for years
out of sheer obstinacy, but it suddenly occurred to him
that, if he did, he wouldn't be bothered by her any more,
and, as he disliked her intensely, it was a cheering
prospect. So that Miss Milton was feeling pleased and
triumphant as she entered the Vicarage drawing-room.
But she was rather surprised when Mrs. Monks came
forward to meet her with outstretched arms and said:

"My dear, I do congratulate you. I think it's simply
wonderful of you."

Of course, it *was* rather wonderful, thought Miss
Milton, because General Moult was notoriously difficult
to interest in any philanthropic scheme. So she smiled
complacently.

"Was that the little surprise you meant?" went on
Mrs. Monks.

"Yes," said Miss Milton. "But how did you know
about it?"

"He told us himself," said Mrs. Monks. "He's in the
garden now. A splendid little man," she added
insincerely.

It occurred to Miss Milton that this was rather an odd
description of the general, but, of course, he was rather

short, and it had been splendid of him to join in with the scheme so promptly.

"Does he have milk or tea for tea?" went on the Vicar's wife.

This again, thought Miss Milton, was a curious question, but she answered from a vague knowledge of the general's habits: "I don't think he ever drinks milk."

"That's all right, then. I gave him tea. My dear, I simply can't tell you how delighted I was to hear the news. It'll make all the difference to your life. I feel certain that you'll never regret it."

How Mrs. Monks did exaggerate, thought Miss Milton. It *was* a triumph, of course, to have got General Moult's name on her list, but it would hardly make "all the difference to her life" and, of course, there was no question of her regretting it.

"Well," she said modestly, "I do feel a little pleased about it."

"I'm sure you do, dear," said Mrs. Monks. "He's in the garden now, you know, playing with his ball."

That, again, was odd, but General Moult was a keen golfer, and there might be some peculiar conformation of ground in the Vicarage garden which assisted him in the practice of some particular shot.

"Go out to him now, dear, won't you?" said Mrs. Monks. "And—I do think tidiness so important, don't you?—tell him to bring in his tea-things and his ball."

Still feeling bewildered, Miss Milton went into the garden. Albert had meantime exhausted its possibilities and made his way out by a hole in the hedge. Miss Milton stood looking in increasing bewilderment at the brightly coloured ball that lay near the summer-house and at the remains of the tea on the summer-house table. The table was covered with crumbs and slops of tea. Cup and saucer lay apart, the saucer half full of tea, a spoon projecting from the cup.

At this moment General Moult appeared through the garden entrance and began making his way up to the Vicarage over the lawn. He'd come to ask the Vicar to lend him a book that the Vicar had on the culture of rhododendrons, in which they were both interested.

Miss Milton looked from him to the ball and the remains of the tea in the greenhouse.

"Mrs. Monks told me to ask you," she said faintly, "to bring in your tea-things and your ball."

General Moult in his turn looked from the gaudily coloured ball to the tea remains, with their strong suggestion of plebeian extraction, and the natural ruddiness of his complexion deepened to purple.

"What!" he roared.

"That's what she told me," said Miss Milton, still more faintly. "I know nothing about it, but she told me to tell you to bring in your tea-things and your ball from the garden."

At this moment Mrs. Monks appeared, beaming ecstatically and leading Albert by the hand. Albert, having found nothing particular to do outside, had wandered in again at the Vicarage front door.

"This is the little boy," said Mrs. Monks to the General, "whom Miss Milton has just adopted."

It was Miss Milton's turn to go purple.

"*What?*" she gasped.

"The little boy whom you've just adopted, Miss Milton," said Mrs. Monks firmly. Really, Miss Milton was behaving very strangely. "Little Albert. Both the Vicar and I think it was a splendid thing to do, and——"

"I've never *seen* him before," said Miss Milton wildly. "I don't know what you're talking about."

"Miss Milton," said Mrs. Monks gravely, "how can you say that? You told me about it yourself just now, and we've just been discussing it together in the drawing-room. I can't think what you mean by suddenly denying your beautiful action like this."

Albert, bored by the scene, slipped out again by the hole in the hedge.

"I never mentioned it to you indoors," almost sobbed Miss Milton. "You must have misunderstood. We were talking about General Moult offering to adopt a poor family."

"*What?*" thundered General Moult. "*Me* adopt a poor family? *Me?* Never heard of such a thing." He turned to Mrs. Monks. "The woman's mad," he said; "stark raving mad. I've suspected it for years. I——"

At this point Albert's mother arrived. She had missed Albert soon after his disappearance and had at once raised a hue and cry. Witnesses bore word of having seen Albert led along the high road by a boy of about eleven. She tracked him to the Vicarage, where a small child bore witness to having seen a boy answering to Albert's description taken in and made much of and fed with a sumptuous tea in the garden. He had, indeed, engaged in a competition of grimaces with him through the hedge.

Albert's mother now confronted Mrs. Monks, arms akimbo, eyes gleaming.

"Where is 'e, that's what I want ter know. Where's my child?"

"I know nothing about your child, my good woman," said Mrs. Monks distantly.

Albert's mother pointed dramatically to the table in the summer-house that bore such ample evidence of

"THIS IS THE LITTLE BOY WHOM MISS MILTON HAS JUST ADOPTED."

Albert's table manners. "Oo's bin 'avin' tea there, then?" she demanded.

"A little boy who's just been adopted by this lady," said Mrs. Monks, pointing to Miss Milton.

"I've never adopted *anyone*," sobbed Miss Milton.

"Well, dear, you distinctly told me you had," said Mrs. Monks. "Most distinctly. You can't change your

"I'VE NEVER SEEN HIM BEFORE," SAID MISS MILTON. "I DON'T
KNOW WHAT YOU'RE TALKING ABOUT."

mind suddenly about an important thing like
that."

" 'Ello, Mum," said a cheerful voice, and Albert was
seen making his way back into the garden through the
hole in the hedge.

There were long and confused explanations, made

longer and more confused by the frequent recriminations between the principals in the drama. Mrs. Monks persisted that Miss Milton had told her she had adopted Albert, Miss Milton persisted that General Monks had offered to adopt a poor family. Albert supported Mrs. Monks in her contention that Miss Milton had adopted him. She'd sent a boy to fetch him. The boy had taken him to her house and had put him in her bed ready for her to cry over, but he didn't like being in bed so he'd come in here. Albert's mother accused them all indiscriminately of child stealing, theft, and murder, and said she'd have the lor on the whole lot of them. The Vicar reluctantly left his sermon and came out to deal with it.

"We must first discover the identity of the boy who fetched the child from his home," he said. "He will probably be able to unravel the mystery. What was the boy like?" he asked Albert.

But even before Albert began to describe the boy, a dark suspicion was forming itself in all their minds.

"William Brown," they said simultaneously, almost before Albert had spoken. "Let's go and find him."

They set off in a body towards the Browns' house.

But William wasn't at home. He was trudging wearily, sorrowfully, up the hill from Hadley. He'd gone down it quickly and joyfully, anxious to impart the glad news to Gert. She was freed from her slavery. Albert had gone. Never again would she have to mind him and wash him and dress him and wrestle with his tantrums. She could go to the pictures or anywhere else she wanted. And, instead of falling on his neck and sobbing out her gratitude, Gert had set on him with tooth and nail. Scratched, bitten, abused, he was making his sad way homewards, reflecting that once again fame seemed to have passed him by . . .

Chapter 7

William the Film Star

THE Outlaws walked slowly down the road discussing the affairs of the moment.

The chief affair of the moment was the visit of a royal personage to Hadley the day before to open some new Municipal Baths. The royal personage had been met by the Mayor and Corporation in ceremonial attire, and the Outlaws had been taken by their parents to witness the sight. The sight had deeply impressed them.

"Dressin' up!" said William enviously. "Grown-ups are always dressin' up, an' then when we want to do it they say no it's babyish an' you'll only make a mess an' that sort of thing. Yet they're always doin' it themselves. Look at the pictures in the newspapers. Parliament bein' opened an' suchlike. Beefeaters an' policemen an' postmen an' judges an' heralds an' men outside cinemas. An' masons. My father's a mason, an' all they do is just dress up in little aprons an' whatnot. An' we've got to go on an' on an' on an' on wearin' ordin'ry clothes day after day an' year after year. No one seems to think we ever want to dress up."

"Yes," agreed Ginger bitterly. "Why should they have all the mayors an' things an' us have nothin'?"

"Yes," agreed William thoughtfully. "Why should they? How do they get mayors?"

"People vote for 'em," said Henry.

"Who votes for 'em?"

"Oh," vaguely, "jus' grown-ups. They vote an' the one that gets the most votes is the Mayor."

"Then why shun't we have one?" said William.

There was silence. No one could think of any reason except Henry, who said doubtfully:

"Well, children never have had 'em."

"That's no reason," said William scornfully. "Everythin's gotter start sometime, hasn't it? I bet once grown-ups hadn't any mayors, an' then someone who was fond of dressin' up started it and then they liked dressin' up so much they kept it on. Well, there's nothin' to stop us startin' it same as grown-ups, is there? I've often thought I'd like to be a peer same as the pictures of the openin' of Parliament, but you've gotter be born one, so we'd better stick to mayors cause you've not gotter be born a mayor."

"Why not?" said Douglas.

"I dunno why not," said William, "but some things like peers an' dukes an' things you've gotter be born, an' other things like mayors an' policemen an' porters an' suchlike you've gotter be made. Well, I don't see why we shun't start children havin' mayors same as grown-ups. I'm sick of grown-ups havin' all the fun. There's nothin' to stop us havin' mayors, anyway, an' I'm jolly well goin' to start it."

"How're you goin' to start it?" demanded Ginger.

"I'm goin' to be Mayor an' you can be the Corp'ration."

They accepted this division of honours as a matter of course. William had always been their leader.

"Lots of people'll want to be in it if we start it," said Douglas.

"They can all be the Corp'ration, then. I'll be the

Mayor an' all the rest can be the Corp'ration."

"What do they *do*?" said Douglas.

"They jus' dress up an' walk about an' have meetin's an' processions an' things," said William vaguely.

"An' they give banquets to people," added Henry.

"Don't anyone give banquets to *them*?" demanded William.

"I 'spect so," said Henry. "They make soup out of turtles. Same as tortoise, you know."

"Well, we can't do that," said William. "Ours hasn't come up after the winter yet, an' I wouldn't make soup of him, even if he had. I bet I shouldn't like it, either—all bits of shell an' stuff."

"Oh, well, they have ordin'ry food, too," said Henry.

"We'll have that, then," said William. "Now I'm Mayor an' the rest of you's the Corp'ration an' we'll start dressin' up to-morrow."

"How'll we dress up?" said Douglas. "They have chains an' robes an' special sort of hats."

"Well, we're not goin' to copy them every way," said William. " 'Sides, we've not gottem. We'll start a new way of dressin' up."

"What way?" said Ginger.

"Well, anythin' we've got," returned William. "We'll all find anythin' we've got an' put that on. I bet it'll turn out a jolly sight better than the grown-ups' way."

It certainly turned out more varied and colourful. William wore the pirate's costume that he had had for a fancy-dress party at Christmas, Ginger wore a discarded red dressing-gown of his mother's, with a saucepan precariously balanced on his head, and Henry wore William's old Red Indian costume, with a dozen or so new feathers (retrieved from Farmer Jenks's hen-run) in its head-dress. Douglas wore his ordinary clothes beneath a handsome cretonne counterpane (whose absence from his bed would, he hoped, escape his mother's notice), and on his head a highly ornamental paper cap saved from his Christmas cracker.

WILLIAM AND THE OUTLAWS MARCHED IN PROCESSION THROUGH THE VILLAGE, GATHERING RECRUITS.

"ANYTHING TO PAY?" THEY ASKED ANXIOUSLY.

Douglas, always a believer in the moral force of the printed word, had written: "Mare and Corprashen" on a large piece of paper and fastened it with drawing-pins to a walking-stick.

Thus equipped and headed by Douglas and his banner, the Outlaws marched in procession through the village the next afternoon. It happened that the juvenile population of the village was feeling bored and ready to welcome any diversion. On hearing that outsiders could be admitted to the Corporation, they enrolled themselves in large numbers.

"Is there anythin' to pay?" they asked anxiously.

"No," William assured them. "You can all be corp'-ration for nothin', but you've gotter dress up."

Joyously they scrounged round for costumes—relics from charades and school plays and fancy-dress parties and pageants. Freddie Parker came in his dragon suit, having forgotten and forgiven the little misunderstanding that had recently given William possession of it for a few crowded hours. Pierrots and cowboys and pages came. Home-made costumes of cardboard, old curtains, tin trays, baskets and tea-cosies came. The entire juvenile population had swelled the "corp'ration" the next day and marched round the village behind William and the banner. The next day there was a Mayoral banquet. The Corporation (fewer of them were in fancy dress to-day, as the more home-made ones had collapsed and the more formal ones had been retrieved by indignant mothers and put away for the next official occasion), marched to the woods and, making a fire, cooked various unsavoury mixtures that they had brought with them. Rain somewhat damped proceedings, but it was a hilarious if sodden party that tramped homewards behind the Mayor and his banner singing

'Pack up your Troubles in your Old Kit Bag." Suddenly, as they passed along the road, two heads shot up over the hedge, and four handfuls of mud were aimed at the Mayor's sacred person. They all fell wide of it—one hit Ginger in the eye—and the whole procession flung itself at the hedge to avenge the insult. The hedge, however, was thick, and the assailants had fled immediately after their attack and had now vanished from sight.

"One of them was Hubert Lane," said Ginger, wiping the mud out of his eyes. "I saw him!"

"Yes, an' the other was Bertie Franks," said Douglas. "I saw him plain."

The Laneites *v.* Outlaws feud had been in abeyance for some time, and the Outlaws were not altogether displeased that it had broken out again.

"They're mad at us bein' a Mayor an' Corp'ration," said William. "They can never think of anythin' themselves an' then they're mad when we do. I bet they come along soon askin' to join an' we jolly well won't have 'em. Not now. Throwin' mud at a Mayor an' Corp'ration! I bet they'd've got executed for that in hist'ry. I often wish I lived in hist'ry. It mus' have been a jolly sight more excitin' than now."

It turned out, however, that the Hubert Laneites had no intention of asking to join the Outlaws' Corporation. Far from it. The news reached them the next morning.

"I say!" Ginger reported excitedly. "Hubert Lane's setting up a Mayor an' Corp'ration of his own."

The Outlaws looked first taken aback and then indignant.

"Cheek!" exploded William and added: "Well, no one'll join his rotten ole Corp'ration, anyway."

But it turned out that William was wrong. Hubert Lane had an adoring mother, who cherished his person

and entered into all his activities with a zest that mos
people considered somewhat excessive, and who had
from the beginning, made his feud against the Outlaw
her own. Douglas brought further news the nex
morning.

"I say! She's made him a real mayor's robe an' hat an
chain, an' she's makin' proper robes for all the Corp'
ration, an' she's givin' 'em a banquet to-morrow with
jellies an' things jus' like a party, an' she says tha
anyone who joins his Corp'ration can come to it."

"Well, I bet no one'll join his ole Corp'ration,'
repeated William stoutly.

At first, indeed, not many of William's supporter:
detached themselves from him, for Hubert wa:
deservedly unpopular, but William had, after all, few
attractions to offer his Corporation compared with
Hubert's. The fame of the banquet spread over the
neighbourhood. There had been fireworks in the garden
afterwards, and presents for all the guests. They had
been asked to enrol their friends in the Corporation
under Hubert and promised a conjuring show the nex
week. The zeal of William's Corporation flagged
somewhat. The weather was cold and wet, so tha
marching in procession and trying to make fires in
the wood lost something of their zest. William held a
meeting in his bedroom, but the noise of the scuffling
and the marks of muddy feet on stairs and passage
caused Mrs. Brown to forbid any further meetings in the
house.

"But I'm the Mayor," protested William indignantly
"I've gotter have a place for my Corp'ration to meet . .
What'd happen to a real mayor, I'd like to know, if his
mother wouldn't let him have a place for his Corp'ratior
to meet?"

"Don't talk such nonsense, William," said Mrs. Brown. "Anyway, you can't have those boys here again and that's flat."

William arranged the next meeting in the old barn, but his was not altogether satisfactory either, as the rain came through the roof and there seemed nothing to do. William, indeed, having tried the idea of Mayor and Corporation and discovered its limitations, would have been quite glad to let it go, had it not been for the rivalry of Hubert Lane. Even Hubert Lane, however, was growing slightly tired of the position. It had been fun to take up William's idea and outshine him, but now that he had outshone him there didn't seem any point in going on with it. And, though there was no doubt that he *had* outshone him, not so many of William's followers had joined him as he had hoped, and it was rather a nuisance not being able to walk abroad without a bodyguard.

So that the whole affair would have fizzled out or ended in a pitched battle between the rival Mayors and Corporations (in which Hubert's would certainly have come off the worse) if it hadn't been for Jimmie Minster. Jimmie Minster was a juvenile film star, beloved by the whole juvenile population of the civilised world. For Jimmie did not belong to the mawkish mother's darling school of child film stars. He was daring and manly and adventurous. He did—and did successfully—all the things that every other boy would like to have done. He boarded pirate ships and bearded thieves in their dens. He was kidnapped and escaped, taking with him all the treasures of his captors. He solved problems that had baffled Scotland Yard experts for years. He always came out on top. His last picture, "Little Sir Rupert", had been a "period" one, and in it Jimmie, as a child

cavalier, with long hair and a broad-brimmed hat and
cloak and mask, had, alone and unaided, held up a coach
and (the plot was very intricate) captured his father'
enemy, who was travelling in it disguised as a
countryman. The picture had been at the Hadley
picture-house the week before, and William and all his
contemporaries had seen it. They had each dreamed
every night since that they were Jimmie Minster, holding
up the coach and capturing the villain.

And now it turned out that Jimmie Minster was the
godson of Miss Appleton who had rented the Hall from
the Botts for the spring, and that he was coming to the
village to spend a day with her. Excitement ran so high
among both children and grown-ups that it would have
driven the subject of Mayor and Corporation from
everyone's mind had it not been for Mrs. Lane. For Mrs
Lane had one of her "sweet ideas" and the "sweet
idea" was that Hubert and his friends, as the young
Mayor and Corporation of the village, should entertain
Jimmie Minster to a banquet. As well as being a "sweet
idea", it would deal the final blow to the pretensions of
William Brown and his followers, which Mrs. Lane was
as eager to accomplish as Hubert himself.

When William heard this, his first plan was to send a
counter invitation to the young film star, but it turned
out that this was too late. Mrs. Lane had written secretly
more than a week before, and had already received a
letter from Jimmie Minster's publicity agent saying that
he would do what he could in the matter. The publicity
agent, as a matter of fact, was delighted with the idea
and thought it almost as "sweet" as Mrs. Lane did. It
was a stunt after his own heart, and he had already
composed for the Press a long and racy description of the
unique banquet at which the youthful Mayor and Cor

oration entertained the youthful film star. Jimmie him-
elf was less enthusiastic, but he was finally bribed and
ajoled into writing a letter of acceptance. It was decided
hat he was to attend the banquet in the costume of his
atest film success—the cloak and mask and broad-
orimmed hat of "Little Sir Rupert".

The Hubert Laneites were jubilant. William and the
emnant of his supporters tried to look indifferent, but it
vasn't easy.

"An' to think we started it," groaned William, "an' it
:nds with *them* havin' Jimmie Minster to a banquet."

They suggested wild ideas in order to get even with
Hubert over it. They suggested asking the Prime Minis-
er, the Pope, the Emperor of Abyssinia, Hitler, and the
1ead of Scotland Yard to a banquet.

They even wrote to some of them but none of them
unswered.

The day of Jimmie's visit arrived. A handful of people
urrived at the Hall gates to see him, but he drove quickly
oy in a closed car and not much of him could be seen.
The majority of people were waiting till the afternoon,
when he was to go from the Hall to the Lanes' house,
lressed in the famous Little Sir Rupert costume. The
Outlaws would have liked to ignore the visit altogether,
out their interest and curiosity were too much for them,
und they decided to wait by the hedge at a point near the
old barn in order to catch a glimpse of him, if possible, as
1e passed. Douglas had been out to reconnoitre, and he
1ad brought back a graphic description of Hubert Lane
n his mayor's robe and chain of office, attended by his
gorgeously attired councillors, waiting at the Lanes'
front door to receive the guest.

"An' our idea!" groaned William for the hundredth
ime.

"An' I bet we shan't even see him, the car'll go by so quick," said Ginger, "an' *they'll* have him all afternoon."

"Oh, shut up," said William.

A large luxurious car came into sight. The Outlaws recognised it as Miss Appleton's.

"That's it," whispered William.

It passed rather slowly, but its occupant was leaning back and the Outlaws could not see him.

"Well, that's not much good," grumbled Ginger. "I din't see anythin' of him at all. Come on."

"Wait a minute," said William.

The car was slowing down. It had come to a stop. The chauffeur left his seat and went to speak to the occupant. Finally he set off alone towards the village. As soon as he had turned the bend, the door of the car opened and a small cloaked figure sprang out and began to run down the road.

On sight of the four faces staring at him over the hedge he stopped.

"I say!" he said breathlessly. "Where can I get through the hedge?"

For a moment the Outlaws were paralysed by amazement. Then William said:

"There's a big hole jus' along there that we generally use."

Without further parley the cloaked figure ran down the road, dived nimbly through the hole—cloak, broad brimmed hat, flowing curls and all—and joined the Outlaws.

"I say!" he said again in a quick business-like voice. "Where can I go so that he won't see me when he comes back with the petrol?"

William, too much taken aback for speech, led the

way over the stile and to the old barn. There Jimmie Minster pulled off hat and wig and looked at them with a grin.

"Won't it be a joke," he said, "when he comes back and finds me not there?"

The Outlaws gazed in stunned reverence at this hero of the screen miraculously come to life.

"I wasn't going to that cracked party," went on Jimmie. "I meant to get out of it somehow from the start. Mayor and Corporation indeed! Set of jackasses! They made me come in these clothes, too, and I've always hated them. Soppy long hair and a hat that comes right down over my eyes. 'Mayor and Corporation of Boyland greets Boy Film Star.'" He uttered an exclamation of disgust. "Makes me sick. The whole lot of 'em make me sick."

"B-but what did you do?" stammered William.

Jimmie grinned.

"Do? I went down to the garage and emptied nearly all the petrol out of the tank. Left enough in to take us half-way. Now he's gone off to the village to get some more petrol and when he comes back," Jimmie chuckled, "he'll find me gone." He looked enviously at the Outlaws. "What were you goin' to do when I saw you in the field?"

"We were goin' to watch you go by," said William, "an' then we were goin' to have a game of Red Indians in the wood."

"Let me come, too," pleaded Jimmie earnestly. "Do. I'm jolly good at Red Indians really, only I hardly ever get a chance. I'll do everything you tell me." His face fell. "I wish I could get out of these beastly clothes."

"I'll lend you mine," said William suddenly.

"I say, that's awfully decent of you! But will yo
do?"

"I'll wear yours."

"But you can't do anything in them," said Jimmie
"They're too tight to run in, and they'd split the momen
you began climbing trees. They're awful."

"Oh, well, never mind," said William. "I'll jus' sta
here in them till you come back."

"It *is* decent of you," said Jimmie again, gratefully
"I'm just longing for a proper game at something. Sure
you don't mind?"

"Yes," said William. "I don't mind a bit. You go on
and play Red Indians."

The exchange of clothing was soon effected. Jimmie'
figure looked less romantic in William's battered
tweeds, but it looked sturdy enough. He leapt about
uttering loud war whoops.

"Come on!" he said. "Let's go to the woods." Again
he glanced with compunction at William, who was jus
buttoning up a black velvet jacket with a white lace
collar. Though a little on the big side, it fitted him fairl
well on the whole.

"Are you *sure* you don't mind?" he said again.

"Yes," said William, "it's quite all right. You run off
an' play Red Indians. I'll be all right here. I'll wait til
you come back."

With another loud whoop, Jimmie raced across the
field, followed by Ginger, Douglas and Henry. It was
clear that he would acquit himself quite creditably as a
Red Indian.

William arranged the wig over his head so that the
long curls hid his own hair, put on the broad-brimmed
feathered hat, and swaggered round the barn. He was
Jimmie Minster. He was Little Sir Rupert. He was

holding up the coach, unmasking the villain. . . . He was driving through the village, leaning nonchalantly back in a car. He was entering the Lanes' house, cheered by a large crowd. He was . . . He stopped. An idea had struck him, struck him so forcibly that for a moment he felt quite breathless. Then he picked up the mask, fixed it over his eyes, slung the cloak over his shoulders, and set off quickly across the field to the road. The car still stood where Jimmie had left it. He walked up to it, opened the door and got in. As he did so the figure of the chauffeur appeared in the distance bent sideways over the weight of a tin of petrol. He went to the back of the car, poured in the petrol, and came to the driving-seat.

"Sorry to 'ave kept you so long, Master Jimmie," he said, glancing at the small figure that lolled back indolently in the corner of the car. "Can't think 'ow I came to get so low in petrol. Not like me at all, it isn't."

He started up the car and began to drive quickly towards the Lanes' home. Surreptitiously William drew the dark wig farther over his head, pulled down the hat, turned up the cloak collar, and fastened the mask more securely to his ears.

The car stopped.

The chauffeur got down and opened the door.

William, his face almost hidden by wig and hat, stepped down from the car.

There was a sudden clicking of cameras, and loud cheers rose on all sides. William didn't feel at all nervous. He was not William Brown masquerading in borrowed plumes, he was not even William Brown scoring off Hubert Lane, he was Jimmie Minster, bored and aloof, acknowledging the plaudits of his admirers. He bowed gracefully and waved a hand, then walked slowly up to the doorway, where Hubert Lane and his councillors stood in their robes of office ready to welcome him. Hubert's face looked hot and shiny with embarrassment, his eyes were glassy, his mouth hung open. It was clear that he was far from happy in his exalted position. Mrs. Lane, arrayed in a new dress of purple velvet, bought specially for the occasion, beamed in the background.

"So this is our famous little guest," she said. "Welcome, welcome, dear boy. Shake hands with him nicely, Hubert."

Hubert shook hands with him nicely and muttered an inaudible sentence in which the word "welcome" could alone be distinguished.

"Hubert is our little local Mayor, dear," went on Mrs. Lane addressing William. "It was quite his own idea. It's charming, isn't it? He was made Mayor because he's the most popular little boy in the neighbourhood. And these are his councillors. Lead Jimmie in, Hubert. I know you two are going to be great friends. I often think that Hubie would have made a great success on the films."

Still glistening with embarrassment, Hubert led William into the dining-room, where the banquet was laid. It was indeed a banquet worth the name—trifle, jellies, fruit salad, blancmange, éclairs, chocolate biscuits, piles of iced cake. William's eyes gleamed behind his mask as he looked at it. The local reporter sat at the far end of the table, and a representative of the publicity agent's stood by the tea-urn, holding a note-book and pencil, ready to take down the little guest's every word.

William was escorted to the seat of honour by Hubert, still glassy-eyed and perspiring. The councillors crowded round.

"Now won't you take off your hat and cape and mask, dear?" cooed Mrs. Lane.

"WON'T YOU TAKE OFF YOUR HAT AND MASK, DEAR?"
COOED MRS. LANE.

William made a vehement gesture of dissent.

"Perhaps you are right, dear," said Mrs. Lane with sigh. "It wouldn't be Little Sir Rupert without then and it's as Little Sir Rupert that we all remember you What a lovely picture that was! Were you nervous whe you were doing it, dear?"

William informed her that he wasn't. He adopted deep husky voice, explaining that he was just recoverin from a bad sore throat. It wasn't in the least suggestive c Jimmie Minster's voice, but neither was it of William's It was merely suggestive of someone with a sore throat William was rather good at hoarse voices. He practise them a good deal, and lived in hopes of some da deceiving his family by one, though he hadn't succeede yet.

"Poor child!" said Mrs. Lane. "What a good thin that it just happened now when you aren't doing picture!"

William agreed that it was.

The councillors took their places at the table, gapin reverently at William. A selection of Hubert's aunt hovered in the distance.

"He doesn't look a bit like he does on the screen, said one.

"They never do," said another.

"Oh, but I think he does," said a third.

All that could be seen of William was his mouth, an even that was shaded by the long curls. The mouth however, was kept fully occupied. Trifle, jelly, blanc mange, disappeared from his plate by magic.

"He's got *quite* a good appetite, hasn't he? murmured one of the aunts.

The shyness of the Hubert Laneites was breakin down. Their joy and exultation at this triumph over thei rivals was increasing each moment. They could not resist giving their guest some inkling of the state of affairs.

"You see," said Hubert, his mouth full of iced cake, "there's a boy here called William Brown, an' he copied us havin' a Mayor an' Corp'ration" (William restrained himself with difficulty at this point), "an' his ole Mayor an' Corp'ration would have liked to have you to a banquet, an' it's jolly snooks for 'em. I bet we'll have a jolly good time shoutin' out at 'em 'Who had Jimmie Minster to a banquet?' I bet that'll make 'em mad all right." He chuckled fatly and the other Hubert Laneites chuckled fatly with him. William gave a hoarse chuckle, and with a great effort kept his fists to himself. "I bet they're out there in the garden now, hidin' and tryin' to look in. I say! Do go an' stand in the window an' show 'em you're here. I bet that'll make 'em mad as mad."

William went to the window and waved his hand airily. Rather to his astonishment the Outlaws actually were there clustered round the gate, laughing and breathless. They had obviously just arrived. With them was Jimmie Minster, still dressed in William's old weeds, his face streaked with mud, his collar awry, his hair standing on end. They had returned to the barn, found William gone, guessed his exploit, and come to reconnoitre. They were all in a state of high glee over the discovery—especially Jimmie, who hung over the gate and shouted "Good ole William!" at the top of his resonant voice.

The Hubert Laneites stared at them from the window.

"William Brown's not there," announced Bertie Franks.

Hubert Lane supplied the explanation of this.

"No, he daren't show his face. Yah!" he shouted derisively through the glass. "Mayor an' Corp'ration indeed! Who's havin' Jimmie Minster to a banquet?"

The real Jimmie Minster put out his tongue and distorted his features into a challenging grimace.

"There's another boy with them," said Mrs. Lane. "A very rough-looking boy, just like the rest of them. He's pulling a very vulgar face. I'll go and send them away."

She went down the path to the gate. Ginger and Douglas and Henry fled, but Jimmie Minster still hung over the gate, grinning at her impudently.

"Go away, little boy," she said severely.

Jimmie adopted a high-pitched squeaky voice.

"Wanter see Jimmie Minster," he squealed.

"Of course you can't see Jimmie Minster," said Mrs. Lane, still more severely. "A dirty untidy little boy like you see Jimmie Minster indeed! I never heard such impertinence. Let me tell you that Jimmie Minster wouldn't even *look* at a dirty little ragamuffin like you. Go away at once."

Jimmie ran off chuckling to join Ginger, Douglas and Henry. "I bet I'll often think of this when I'm doing some beastly soppy picture," he chuckled as he ran down the road with the three.

Meanwhile William was beginning to think that it was time that the proceedings came to an end. He'd enjoyed the banquet, he'd collected many inane remarks of Hubert's that would come in as useful weapons in time to come, and he had so far evaded discovery, but he felt that he'd wrung as much entertainment from the situation as it was capable of yielding and it was time he went home. There was still a strong element of danger. He still might be discovered at any moment, and, if that happened, surrounded as he was on all sides by his enemies, he would come off rather badly. One of

Hubert's aunts was still persisting that he didn't look a bit like he did in his pictures.

"I know his mouth's all you can see," she said, "but even that looks quite different to me."

"It's the make-up," put in another aunt with an air of deep wisdom. "They have to put a lot of make-up on, and it alters the shape of their features."

"He's shyer than I'd thought he'd be, too," said another. "You can hardly drag a word out of him."

"It's that awful throat he's got," said another. "I wonder Miss Appleton let him come out with it. Funny that she never mentioned it when I met her in the village this morning."

"He hasn't got the *charm* he has on the screen," sighed the first.

"Ah, the glamour of the footlights!" said Mrs. Lane. "How often is that the case!"

"I wish he'd tell us more about the life of the studio," said the second aunt. "What he's told us does sound so odd."

William, pressed on all sides, had given in his deep hoarse voice a somewhat strange account of life in a film studio. Describing a normal day there, he had said that the actors all had breakfast together at eight o'clock, acted till lunch-time, had lunch together, then went for walks till tea-time, had tea together, then acted again in the evening. He added that they sometimes played football or cricket in the afternoon instead of going for walks. He said that the actors were told the story of the picture and then made up their parts as they went along.

"Most interesting," said the second aunt, "and somehow quite different from what I'd imagined."

"Quite different from what I've read in books about it, too," said the third aunt rather grimly. She didn't for

a moment suspect that William was Jimmie Minster, but
she was beginning to have a strong suspicion that Jimmie
Minster was pulling their legs.

"I expect the procedure differs in the various
studios," said Mrs. Lane, passing the chocolate biscuits
again to William.

The second aunt looked at him soulfully. She thought
the mouth a little disappointing (where were those
wistful cupid-like lines that had brought tears into her
eyes in "Somebody's Boy" and "The Little Waif"?) but
she was adoring the hat and curls and cloak and lace
collar and her memories of Little Sir Rupert at the
Hadley Palais de Luxe.

William made a determined effort.

"I think I'd better be goin' now," he said in his hoarse
voice. "I've gotter be back early."

"Oh but, dear," protested Mrs. Lane, "your god-
mother's sending the car for you, you know. You must
wait till the car comes. Besides we've got a little surprise
for you. I know Hubert isn't a famous actor like you
because, for one thing, of course, he doesn't need
to earn his living, but he really has talent, and I want
you to hear him recite before you go. Now Hubert
dear."

Hubert, pallid and glistening, rose from his seat, went
to the centre of the room, struck an attitude, and began
to recite.

"It was the schooner *Hesperus* that sailed the
    wintry sea
  And the skipper had brought his little daughter
      to bear him company."

William watched and listened with an attentiveness
that deeply gratified Hubert, who little knew that he was

cherishing every word, every gesture for future use. He clapped loudly and enthusiastically at the end. It had been indeed a veritable treasure trove for the Laneites *v.* Outlaws feud.

"And now, dear," said Mrs. Lane, "there's one more little surprise for you. Hubert, dear."

Again Hubert rose, went to a side table, took a paper parcel and handed it to William with a low bow. William opened the parcel. It was a small model aeroplane such as he had always longed to possess. So pleased was he that he almost forgot to use the new husky voice in expressing his thanks.

"Come an' show it at the window," said Hubert. "I bet that ole William Brown's hidin' about somewhere an' tryin' to see what's goin' on. He's been wantin' an aeroplane like this for ever so long. He was savin' up his money for it, an' then he got it all took off him for breakin' a window." Hubert sniggered maliciously. "Go on, hold it up an' let him see it if he's hidin' anywhere round, an' I bet he is. He was as sick as sick 'cause we had you to a banquet an' not him. Go on. Wave it round, an' let him see it."

William obeyed, and Hubert danced an ungraceful war-dance beside him, grinning derisively and shouting: "Yah, ole William Brown!" The other councillors took up the cry "Yah, ole William Brown! Who's having Jimmie Minster to a banquet? Who's got an aeroplane like the one you wanted an' couldn't get? Yah—*boo*!"

Mrs. Lane smiled fondly in the background.

"And now, Jimmie dear," she said, "you'll take off the hat and mask and cloak—won't you?—and let us see the real Jimmie."

They all cheered and crowded round him, putting out willing hands to assist in the disrobing. William looked

round desperately for escape. To his relief he saw Miss
Appleton's car drawing up at the door.

"No," he said with husky urgency, "no, I mus' go
now. Tell you what. I'll do it when I'm in the car jus' at
the gate, shall I? That'll be better. You see," he added
mysteriously, "I *mus'* stay like I am till I'm right out of
the house."

"Professional etiquette, I expect," said the first aunt
vaguely.

"A sense of the dramatic," explained the second.

"Very odd," said the third.

HE WHIPPED OFF HAT, MASK, AND WIG, AND THE HOMELY
FEATURES OF WILLIAM BROWN WERE REVEALED.

THEY RUSHED FORWARD WITH YELLS OF RAGE.

But William didn't stay to argue. Thanking them with desperate hoarseness for the entertainment, he went to the front door and got into the car. Mayor, Corporation, aunts and Mrs. Lane came out to wave him off.

"You won't forget?" said Mrs. Lane coyly. "At the gate."

"No," shouted William.

He whispered a word to the chauffeur. The car drew out of the gate and stopped in the road.

Mayor, Corporation, aunts and Mrs. Lane stood watching expectantly.

Little Sir Rupert leaned out of the window of the car.

He whipped off hat, mask, cloak, and wig.

The grinning homely features of William Brown were revealed.

With yells of rage the Hubert Laneites rushed forward but it was too late. The car had started and was already on its way.

The Hubert Laneites pursued it ineffectually down the road, shouting angrily, tripping over their robes of office in their haste. William continued to hang out of the window.

He waved the aeroplane triumphantly.

Above the Hubert Laneites' howls of rage his voice could be heard in imitation of Hubert's squeaky singsong:

"It was the schooner *Hesperus* that sailed the
      wintry sea
   The skipper had brought his little daughter to
      bear him company."

*   *   *

At the hole in the hedge William stopped the car and made his way across the fields to the old barn, where Jimmie and the Outlaws awaited him.

"Well, I've had a jolly good time," said Jimmie, as they changed clothes. "I don't know about you."

An ecstatic look came over William's face as the memories of the afternoon marshalled themselves before him. "Yes, I have," he said simply. "A *jolly* good time."

Chapter 8

William the Globe-Trotter

WILLIAM sat on a stile, his elbows on his knees, his chin in his hands, sunk in gloomy thought. Everything he had undertaken lately seemed to have gone wrong. He had entered upon his last undertaking with high hopes. It had seemed an excellent and easy means of making money, and William, who, like most people, found his income insufficient to meet his needs, was always on the look-out for an easy means of making money. He still considered that it was a good idea in itself, and that its failure was due simply to bad luck.

In the neighbourhood of William's home there were several mansions—chiefly Elizabethan—that were open to the public on certain days of the week. The public paid a shilling or two shillings, as the case might be, and for that sum were escorted over the mansion by a guide and bidden to mark its beauties and points of interest. William did not see why this system should be confined to the stately homes of England. His own home, though comparatively lacking in stateliness, contained some undeniable points of interest. There was the hole that Jumble had made in the hall carpet (now covered by a rug), the baluster that had had a piece knocked out where William had lost control in sliding down, the frog that he had (not very successfully) stuffed, the damp patch in the bathroom wall where a pipe had burst, and the attic where one could get out on to the roof or make ghostlike noises by shouting into the water cistern. William, of course, realised that these were not equal in general interest to priests' holes and carved corbels and picture galleries and tapestries, but he considered that they *were* definitely interesting.

He did not intend to charge two shillings or even one shilling for entrance. He thought that a steady flow of visitors at a penny each, one or two afternoons a week, would prove a pleasant and easy source of income. He did not for a moment expect that his parents would agree to this, but he did not see why they should know anything about it. His mother went every Wednesday afternoon to help at a Welfare Centre, and he thought that if he threw the house open to the public during the hours of her absence no possible harm could be done. With vague memories of a recent visit to a neighbouring Elizabethan manor, he imagined himself conducting a small orderly party of sightseers from room to room, explaining the points of interest, answering a few timid questions, and finally ushering them out of the front door again. Perhaps some of them would even give him a tip. He'd be able to buy that football that he'd seen in Hadley as well as the motor boat. He might get as much as five shillings a week by it. He couldn't think why he hadn't tried it before. . . .

The next Wednesday afternoon he waited till his mother had safely departed for her Welfare Centre, then fetched from his bedroom the notice that he had printed the night before on a page from his arithmetic exercise book. "Open to the Publik Wensday Afternoon Entunce one penny," and hung it on the gate. That done, he took his seat by the drawing-room window to watch for clients. Even now, of course, the coast was not quite clear. The visitors must not ring the bell, for, if they did, the housemaid would answer it and summarily send them about their business. William, therefore, had left the front door ajar, so that he could intercept them before they reached it and, after collecting their pennies, start the sightseeing tour. He held a small tin in which to collect their fees and sat with his eyes fixed on the gate reciting his lecture to himself. "Under this rug you see a hole in the carpet made by Jumble. There was a sort of rose in the pattern and he kept trying to get it out. I knocked that bit off the balusters with my head. I made a jolly big lump on my head—nearly as big as a football. I got how to stuff that frog out of a book. They always smell a bit. You can't help it . . ."

Quarter of an hour passed; half an hour passed. Only two people came along the road, and neither of them stopped to read the notice. William became bored. He decided to go for a walk, and, whistling for Jumble, set off by the side door, quite forgetting that the front door was still ajar and the notice still on the gate. He was away longer than he had meant to be and returned to find the place in an uproar, his mother distracted. A passing tramp had obeyed the notice, entered by the open front door, and departed with the silver vases from the drawing-room mantelpiece, duly leaving a penny on the hall table. In vain did William protest his good intentions, his desire to restore the fortunes of his family and make them all millionaires. His excuses were brushed aside and retribution sternly dealt out to him.

And that led to Miss Milton. If it hadn't been for the affair of the tramp, his mother would not have insisted on his joining Miss Milton's Educational Play Guild.

Miss Milton was one of those unfortunate beings who are cursed with a social conscience. She was always devising schemes for the betterment of mankind, and failure only spurred her on to further efforts. Her recent agitation for the adopting of poor families by well-to-do ones had proved a signal failure, but Miss Milton was not discouraged. Far from it. She at once set to work to devise further schemes. The latest was the Educational Play Guild for Children. It was to be held on Wednesday afternoons, and Mrs. Brown immediately enrolled William, on the grounds that then, at any rate, she'd know what he was doing while she was at the Welfare. William protested passionately against this. He didn't want to be educated. He was educated every day in school, wasn't he? Well, it wasn't fair on the masters in school to start messing about with his education out of school. He'd be getting on too fast for them, and then there wouldn't be anything else left to teach him, and he'd have to leave school because of knowing everything, and then she'd have him at home all day for the rest of his life, and how would she like that? And, anyway, he didn't want to play—not like that. He didn't believe in mixing up play and education. He didn't think it was right. And he didn't like Miss Milton. He never had and he never would. And he didn't want to go to her rotten old play guild. But it was all in vain.

With frequent references to the silver vases Mrs. Brown remained firm in her decision. William was to attend Miss Milton's Educational Play Guild. All verbal persuasion having proved useless, William turned his attention to the symptoms of various diseases, but his mother was accustomed to this, and, the more realistic his performances, the less was she impressed. The next Wednesday, therefore, William, washed and brushed

and dressed in his best suit, was delivered by Mrs. Brown
at the Village Hall, the headquarters of the Educational
Play Guild, on her way to the Welfare. She was to call for
him on her way back. It was, she considered, providen-
tial that the Village Hall lay on her way to the Welfare.
After those silver vases, she'd never have known a
moment's peace at the Welfare again with William
ranging at large . . .

A small party of depressed-looking children were
assembled in the hall. Most of them had been sent by the
parents under stress of the same emotions as had
inspired Mrs. Brown. If they were in the Village Hall,
being educated by Miss Milton, at least they couldn't be
anywhere else doing anything else. Miss Milton was
bright and alert, her eyes shining with purpose. This, she
felt sure, looking at the glum faces around her and
mistaking their glumness for earnestness, was going to
be the most successful of all her philanthropic schemes.

"Now, children," she said briskly, "the first thing
we're going to play at is Birds and Flowers. Each of the
boys will be a bird and each of the girls a flower. You'll
have a lovely game, and at the same time learn all about
the beautiful bird and flower kingdoms."

She proceeded to assign various birds to the boys and
various flowers to the girls. William received the news
that he was a tom-tit without enthusiasm. Without
enthusiasm also he received a detailed description of his
appearance and habits. He was, he was told, a valuable
destroyer of pests, fond of fat and coconut. He did not
emigrate. He nested in any convenient hole near the
house or along the lanes, using moss, wool, hair and
feathers. His tail and wings were blue, his back a
yellowish green. His song lasted all the year round.

William listened to all this with a glassy stare. Miss

Milton went on to the others and told them, one by one, their characteristics as birds and flowers. She then gave them little cards with their characteristics written down.

"And now we'll have a jolly game," she said brightly. "I'll give you five minutes to learn what's on the cards, then I'll pin the cards on your backs and you can go round and ask each other questions about the bird or flower you represent and look on the back to see if the answers are right. Won't that be fun?"

"Yes, but what's the game?" asked William.

"That *is* the game, dear," said Miss Milton patiently. "Think what fun you'll have asking each other questions and then seeing if the answers are right! And there's another thing that I'm going to tell you. Something *very* exciting indeed, so exciting that I really don't think I ought to tell it to you just on top of the new game." She made a pause in which anticipation was supposed to stretch itself on tenterhooks, then continued. "I thought that later on we'd have a little party for your parents, to show them what jolly times we have, and you could all dress up as the birds and flowers you represent and each say a little rhyme."

"What rhyme'll I say?" demanded William.

"Well," said Miss Milton modestly, "I haven't got everything quite planned out yet, but I did think of a nice little rhyme for tom-tit.

" 'About the garden I do flit,
      Tom-tit am I, I am tom-tit.' "

William considered this in silence for a few moments, then said:

"If I've gotter be a bird, I'd sooner be a vulture than a tom-tit."

"Why, dear?" said Miss Milton.

"I'd sooner be a bird that eats dead men than one that jus' eats coconuts."

Miss Milton blenched.

"I don't think that's very nice, dear," she said faintly.

"I'd sooner be a vulture than any other sort of bird," insisted William. "They know when people are dyin' an' they hover round 'em an' then swoop down an' start eatin' 'em straight away. I'd like to do that. It'd be a jolly sight more excitin' than singin' in gardens an' suchlike."

"Don't, dear," said Miss Milton. "I think that's horrid. No, you're a dear little tom-tit, and you've got a dear little rhyme to say about yourself."

"I bet I could make up one jus' as good about a vulture," said William. He was silent for a moment, staring thoughtfully into the distance, then: "Yes, I knew I could. I'm jolly good at makin' up po'try.

> "'I swoop right down on 'em, and then
> Dead men I eat, I eat dead men.'"

"No, William," said Miss Milton very firmly, "we won't have any more of that. It isn't nice at all. It really isn't. You ought to try and fill your mind with beautiful thoughts, William——"

"Well, a vulture *is* a beautiful thought," persisted William. "It's a jolly sight beautifuller than a tom-tit any day."

"We won't talk any more about that for the present," said Miss Milton. "Let's talk about our future arrangements. I thought that perhaps next week we might each choose a great character in history, find out all we can about him or her, and tell each other. That will be great fun, won't it?"

She smiled brightly round the assembly. No one spoke except William who said:

"Mine's Guy Fawkes."

"But he wasn't a good man, dear," said Miss Milton.

"He was the only one that did *us* any good, anyway," said William firmly. "He started bonfires an' fireworks, an' that's a jolly sight more than any of the others did. Messin' about with wars an' rebellions an' things, an' never thinkin' of anyone but themselves! He thought of givin' other people a bit of pleasure, anyway. I bet he got jolly bored himself in November thinkin' Christmas was never comin', so he started fireworks an' things to cheer people up, an' I think it was jolly kind of him."

"But William," said Miss Milton, "you're quite wrong. You——"

"I'm goin' to have him, anyway," interrupted William, "an' I bet I can make up a piece of po'try about him, too." Again he considered for a moment then: "Yes, I knew I could.

" 'You can make my moustaches with burnt
        corks,
    Guy Fawkes I am, I am Guy Fawkes.' "

"Nonsense, William," said Miss Milton, who was beginning to regret having put her poem about the tom-tit into that particular form. "Well, I think perhaps we won't have historical characters, after all. We'll have—we'll have adventurers. Each of you must choose someone who'd had some great adventure and tell each other all about him or her next week. Now we'll go on with our bird and flower game."

An hour or so later Mrs. Brown collected a dejected boy from the Village Hall.

"We've had such a jolly time," Miss Milton assured her brightly, "haven't we, children?"

A groan, which she took to be a murmur of assent, broke from the little assembly.

"This time next week, then," went on Miss Milton. "And all get busy with your adventures."

William set off moodily homeward beside his mother.

"I'm so glad you've enjoyed it, dear," said Mrs. Brown.

"Enjoyed it?" echoed William indignantly. "Enjoyed it? Me? Enjoyed it? It's been awful. All about tom-tits and stuff. It's jus' about turned me sick. If I've gotter go there every Wednesday afternoon I—well"—darkly—"I shun't be surprised if I died."

"Nonsense," said Mrs. Brown, "and, anyway, William, after those vases——"

"Those vases!" echoed William. "I'd rather've gone to prison for 'em straight off. *She* wouldn't't've been there anyway, goin' on about tom-tits an' things. I wouldn't't've minded goin' to prison. It'd've been fun filin' my way out with a file or diggin' an underground passage out same as people in books. 'Sides, you go on as if *I'd* stolen the vases. I don't see how I can help other people stealin' things when I'm not even there to stop 'em. I s'pose you think everythin' in the world that's stolen's my fault jus' 'cause I wasn't there to stop it. Well, come to that, it's everyone's fault, so why shun't everyone that doesn't steal be put in prison 'cause they've not been able to stop people stealin' same as I couldn't? Then that'd jus' leave thieves out of prison an' what sense is that?"

"William, dear," said Mrs. Brown mildly, "I don't know what you're talking about, but you do talk the most dreadful nonsense."

"It's not nonsense," said William. "Have I to go nex' Wednesday?"

"Of course," said Mrs. Brown. "I expect you'll get to like it when you get used to it."

"Why should I?" challenged William. "You might jus' as well say people'd get to like poison if they got used to it. They'd get to like it when they're dead, p'r'aps," he continued with heavy sarcasm, "an' that's the only way I'll get to like her an' her ole tom-tits."

They had reached home now, and Mrs. Brown, who hadn't been listening to him, said, "Yes, dear," vaguely, "and don't forget to wipe your feet on the mat."

William snorted defiantly but wiped his feet on the mat, washed his hands and face, and made an excellent tea.

He had meant to show his scorn of the whole proceeding by refusing to give any thought to the subject of adventure, but it was a subject that had always attracted him, and he found his thoughts turning to it despite himself.

"Mother," he said suddenly, "what d'you think's the greatest adventure that's ever been done?"

Mrs. Brown considered.

"Well, I don't know, dear. What about the discovery of America?"

"No, I don't think much of that," said William, as he thoughtfully munched a piece of bread and jam. "Whenever I do try chewin' gum I'm always swallowin' it by mistake, an', anyway, it's only made more dates to learn."

"Well, then, the discovery of the North Pole."

"No, I don't think much of that, either. They jus' went to a place that was there all the time. Anyone could do that. An' it wasn't any use when they got there—all snow an' ice an' stuff. No, I don't think much of that."

"Well, that's all I can think of," said Mrs. Brown firmly, "and, William dear, do try to eat more slowly. It's not good for you to bolt your food like that."

"Well, I've gotter keep my strength up after an awful afternoon like that, haven't I?" William justified him-

"WILLIAM, DEAR," SAID MRS. BROWN, "DO TRY TO EAT MORE SLOWLY."

self, stretching out for the last piece of bread and jam. His mind was still busy with the subject of adventure, but he could think of none that really interested him.

"What about aeroplanes?" said his mother.

"No," said William bitterly, "they look like birds an' I'm sick of birds. 'Tom-tit I am,' " he quoted with an expression of nausea.

That evening, however, he happened to pick up a library book of Robert's and was soon absorbed in it, deaf and blind to everything around him. It was about a man who had travelled ten thousand miles with two ponies from Buenos Aires to New York, beset by danger on every side—crocodiles, electric eels, vampire bats, and fever. It was the sort of adventure in which William's soul delighted—one man pitting himself alone against gigantic hostile forces.

"Here! Give me that!" said Robert, snatching the book out of his hand indignantly, for it seemed to lower his, Robert's, dignity that a kid like William should read and enjoy his book.

"*Gosh!*" said William, still bemused by the spell of the book. "Fancy him doin' all that! Two an' a half years at it, too! An' all alone! Wasn't it a wonder he wasn't killed?"

"Shut up and mind your own business," said Robert, sitting down and burying himself in the book.

William was not at all abashed by the rebuff, for it was Robert's usual mode of address to him and any other sort would have embarrassed both of them.

"I bet he felt a bit scared leadin' those ponies across those swayin' bridges over canyons," went on William.

Robert, deep in the book again, made no answer.

William spent that evening in a sort of dream. That was the adventure for him—to go ten thousand miles through the dangers of desert and jungle all alone but for his faithful ponies. Already he was beginning to feel that he, and not the author, had performed the feat. Anyway, if one person could do it, another could. Two and a half years. Well, that wouldn't matter. If he was away two and a half years, at any rate he'd miss school and that awful stuff of Miss Milton's on Wednesday afternoon. That alone would be worth being away two and a half years. Yes, he'd do it. It was an adventure after his own heart. It would need a little adjusting, of course. He couldn't very well go from Buenos Aires to New York, as he wasn't at Buenos Aires to start with. And he might find it difficult to get two ponies. Still, William was not the boy to give up a perfectly good plan because of a few initial difficulties. He'd take Jumble instead of the two ponies. Jumble, being only a small dog of highly mixed breed, could not, of course, serve the same purpose as the ponies, but he'd be company. And he wouldn't bother to carry tents or anything like that. He'd sleep in barns and under hedges like a tramp. He'd often thought he'd like to try being a tramp. The more he considered the project, the more alluring it became.

The money, of course, would be a difficulty, because he'd only got twopence halfpenny, and even William's optimism didn't think that that would take him far, but again, like a tramp, he would beg his way. He'd once read in the papers that beggars made a lot of money. Some of them even kept motor cars. Perhaps he'd come home a millionaire. And, of course, as he couldn't ride he'd have to walk, which was really better, he decided as he could go across country and over fields, whereas, if he'd had ponies, he'd have had to keep to the road. For since he couldn't ride from Buenos Aires to New York he'd decided to walk round the world. He'd walk round

he world with Jumble. It was the next best thing to
iding from Buenos Aires to New York with two ponies.
t seemed even to have some points of superiority.

He didn't know quite how many miles it was round the
vorld, but more, he was sure, than ten thousand. And
he'd be walking instead of riding, so it would take even
onger than he'd have taken riding. Perhaps about five
years. Well, he wouldn't mind being away for five years.
He'd miss school, he'd miss (he scowled with fierce
ffort as he did the mental sum) two hundred and sixty of
hose awful Wednesday afternoons of Miss Milton's.
That would be worth it alone. He'd just start off and go
n a straight line and he'd get back to where he started
rom. Well, the world was round—wasn't it?—so it
tood to reason he would. He'd come to one or two seas,
f course, but he'd just have to work his way across them
s straight as he could. People in books always worked
heir way across seas . . . He'd work it as a cabin boy or
teward or mate or something. Perhaps he'd be able to
ave them from pirates or discover a leak in the ship just
n time. They'd be so grateful that they'd make him
Captain. He had a glorious vision of himself standing on
 bridge, issuing orders or training his cannon on to a
lack ship with the skull and cross-bones flying from the
nast. Then he'd sail to some undiscovered island and
nd a lot of hidden treasure. He pulled himself up
harply. He must stick to the adventure in hand. He was
oing to walk round the world, not sail to discover
idden treasure. That could come later . . .

He spent the next morning collecting his things—a
ompass that he'd once got out of a cracker and that
vould help him to steer a straight course, a penknife
vith something for getting the stones out of horses'
oofs that he had always felt would come in useful

sometime, some dog biscuits for Jumble, his bow and
arrows (he might, he thought, with luck, kill a rabbit or
hare and, anyway, they'd be a defence against wild
animals), a length of string, some marbles and a piece of
putty, because he'd had them in his pocket for so long
that he'd have felt lost without them. He made a particularly large and hearty lunch, as it might be the last square
meal that he'd have for several years, then, waiting till
his mother was safely lying down and the cook and
housemaid busy in the kitchen, crept round the larder to
forage for a few provisions. They could hardly grudge
him that, he thought, considering that they wouldn't
have to pay anything more for his food for five years.

He filled a large paper bag with a mixture of apple pie
cold meat, breakfast sausage, cold potato, blancmange
and currant cake. It would, he imagined, be enough for
the first few days. Then he'd have to begin begging his
way. He took a last look at his home, feeling a little
wistful at the thought that it might be many many years
before he saw it again. The wistfulness of this thought
was mingled with jubilation, however, for when he came
back he'd be famous and they'd have to treat him a bit
different. Even Robert would have to be polite to him.
He couldn't imagine Robert being polite to him, but the
fact remained that people *would* have to be polite to
someone who'd walked round the world. There'd be no
going to that awful thing of Miss Milton's any more.
They'd be jolly sorry they'd ever made him.

"Come on, Jumble," he said and set off, feeling
somewhat regretful at not having a more dramatic
departure. He'd like to have had his whole family
weeping on the doorstep, but, of course, if they'd been
there they wouldn't have wept and they'd have stopped
him going, so he realised that that was impossible.

Jumble, of course, did not know that he was leaving home on a glorious adventure and behaved in his usual undignified fashion, snapping at flies, romping over flower-beds, and worrying William's shoe-laces.

William walked a little way down the road and then stood, considering the situation. There were two stiles on either side of the road exactly opposite each other. It was obviously the place to begin. He'd start out by one stile and then in five years' time or so he'd come back by the other. Well, he'd have to if he went straight round the world, following his compass as he meant to.

He set his compass at the stile on the left and set off across country. He walked over the field, through a hole in a hedge and across another field, keeping in a straight line. He managed this for some time, and at last began to feel tired and hungry, so sat down under a hedge and opened his bag of provisions. He'd meant them to last several days, of course, but he might as well make a start on them now. It would make the bag less heavy to carry and help to keep his strength up. He'd only just eat a very little. He ate absently, giving bits to Jumble occasionally, his thoughts far away in a pleasant dreamland in which he wrestled successfully with crocodiles, electric eels, tigers, lions, and returned to his native land amidst the plaudits of his countrymen. He gave a start as his eyes fell upon the empty bag. Gosh! He'd eaten it all. He hadn't meant to. Well, he'd just have to start begging his way when he got hungry again, that was all. He'd be reaching the sea soon and then he'd be a cabin boy or something, and they'd give him his food.

It must be jolly late. He'd been walking for hours and hours. Funny it wasn't getting dark. A church clock startled him by striking three. Crumbs! Only *three*. He'd thought he must almost be at the sea by now. The old church clock was probably wrong. He gave Jumble his dog biscuits, got up, and set off again, Jumble trotting happily at his heels. He'd go on a bit longer. He'd be sure to get to the sea soon. He found himself on the outskirts of a wood, but made his way through the hedge and walked straight on. There were little nesting-boxes fastened on to the trees, and at intervals small tables, covered with nuts and crumbs of cake. William, who was feeling hungry again, cleared each as he came to it. The nuts were quite good and the cake crumbs not too stale. On one there were some pieces of apple and these, too, William ate gratefully. There seemed to be some providence that looked after adventurers. Perhaps there was something in fairy tales, after all, and he'd come under a sort of spell. He wouldn't have to bother about begging his way, of course, if he found little tables of food set for him all round the world. He walked on, singing untunefully as he went. The spell was abruptly broken by a young man with a very pale face, nearly all nose, and a multi-coloured pullover, who came down one of the woodland paths, carrying a nesting-box in one hand and a coconut in the other.

"What are you doing here?" he said sternly to William.

"Me?" said William. "I'm jus' walkin' through."

He spoke coldly and distantly. The young man would not know, of course, that he was addressing one of the world's great heroes, one who was walking round the entire world alone with a dog, braving innumerable dangers.

"Walking through!" exploded the young man angrily. "Tramping through like a herd of elephants, shouting like a crowd of hooligans. Do you know what this is?"

"HOW DARE YOU COME HERE WITH THAT BOW AND ARROW?"

"No," said William calmly.

"It's a bird sanctuary," shrilled the young man. "A bird sanctuary. A sanctuary of peace and quiet for my feathered friends. It's my life's work. I never come here except in goloshes so as not to disturb them. And you— *you*—come tramping and shouting—with *that*." Trembling with rage, he pointed to the bow and arrows that William carried under his arm. "How *dare* you come into my sanctuary with that?"

"I'm not shootin' birds with it," explained William patiently. "I've got it for wild beasts an' suchlike. An' for food. In some of the places I'm goin' through I shan't have any food except what I kill. I jolly well wouldn't waste my arrows on birds. I've only got two an' sometimes when you've shot 'em it's jolly hard to find 'em again. I'm goin'——"

At this minute Jumble, who had disappeared into the undergrowth some minutes before, reappeared, leaping about excitedly and worrying a stick. The young man shrank back, white with horror.

"A *dog*!" he gasped. "A *dog* rampaging about in my bird sanctuary! The work of months undone. One of the chaffinches was nearly tame and—how *dare* you bring a dog here?"

"Well, I couldn't get two ponies," explained William, "and I'd gotter have something. He'll be company in some of those wild places I'm goin' to. I've gotter go over deserts with only oases an' things to eat" (William's geography was of a somewhat scanty description) "an' over rivers full of crocodiles an'——"

But the young man was not interested in William's round-the-world tour.

"Didn't you see the notice at the gate?" he demanded.

"No, I didn't come in by the gate," explained William. "You see, I can't go round by gates an' things. I've gotter go straight on or I'll not come back to the place I started from. Stands to reason, doesn't it? When I come to houses an' places I can't get straight through, I'll have to go round 'em, of course, but places I can get through, same as hedges an' woods an' suchlike, I have to. It's goin' to take me years an' years, anyway, so I can't go wastin' my time readin' notices an'——"

"*Will* you be quiet?" snapped the young man, struggling desperately against the turgid tide of William's eloquence. "I don't know what you're talking about and I don't care. All I know is that you're trespassing on my land and disturbing my bird sanctuary, and if you aren't gone in two minutes I'll send for the police. Now get off with you! There's the gate." He pointed in the direction from which William had come.

"I can't go that way," explained William patiently. "That's the way I've come. I've gotter go straight on same as I told you. Well, I *was* goin' straight on if you'd not come, interruptin' me an' wastin' my time. I'd've been miles on by now if it'd not been for you. Anyway, I've got as much right in a bird sankcherry as anyone, 'cause I'm a sort of tom-tit. But I wouldn't stop in it now, not even if you asked me. Come on, Jumble."

He walked on his way with stolid dignity, Jumble trotting at his heels. The young man stared after him, helpless and open-mouthed, then tiptoed along to the bird tables and stood gazing down at their empty surfaces with a seraphic smile.

Meanwhile William plodded on through the wood, across a field, along a lane, and down a road that seemed to be taking him in a fairly straight direction. He was thinking about the bird sanctuary. Bird sanctuary

indeed! He'd always felt bitter about what he considere
the undue importance given to birds. People making
fuss of them and putting out nuts and things for them a
over the place. You might starve for all they cared a
long as *birds* had plenty of coconuts and stuff. He knew
several elderly ladies, who would drive him indignantl
out of their gardens and to whom it would never eve
occur to offer him refreshment, but who regularly se
feeding trays and coconuts for birds. Bird sanctuar
indeed! Why not a boy sanctuary? A boy sanctuary. I
was a novel and intriguing idea. William set to work to
plan its details. A wood entirely devoted to boys—
grown-ups not allowed to enter. Tables of chocolate
cream and humbugs and lollypops at intervals. Bo
baths of lemonade and orange squash. Cream bun
hanging from trees. Instead of nesting-boxes, toy
placed against all the trees—motor boats, bows and
arrows, electric trains, cricket sets, footballs.

A boy sanctuary. He wondered no one had eve
thought of it before. Fancy taking all this trouble al
these years over bird sanctuaries and no one ever havin;
thought of a boy sanctuary! It would be quite easy to
arrange. He'd have done it himself if he hadn't just se
out on his five years' walk round the world. He almos
wished he'd put off his walk till he'd tried the boy
sanctuary. But no. Even the boy sanctuary couldn'
compensate for those awful Wednesday afternoons with
Miss Milton. The road bent sharply round to the right
That wouldn't do. He must keep straight on. He climbed
a fence and began to walk over a field. There were oat:
or corn or barley or something growing in it, but William
couldn't help that. He didn't mean to go round anything
that he could possibly go through. He plodded on, still
pondering on the subject of the boy sanctuary, Jumble

isking about among the green shoots, and had almost
reached the other end of the field, when he heard an
angry shout and glanced up to see a pair of gaiters and
hobnailed boots descending upon him. His gaze rose
from the hobnailed boots to meet the glare of a pair of
angry eyes in a red whiskered face, and he recognised,
too late, his old enemy, Farmer Jenks.

"Now I've got ye, ye young varmint," said the new-
comer, and, seizing hold of William before he had time
to dodge, pummelled him, boxed his ears, and threw
him over the fence into the road.

William sat up and rubbed his head. His assailant was
walking off down the road still muttering angrily to
himself.

"All right," said William, "you wait! You just wait!
You'll be only too glad to let me walk over your ole fields
when I come back famous."

Anyway, he'd got across the field and that was the
great thing. He picked himself up, rubbed his head
again, wondered whether to retrieve his cap, which had
fallen where the farmer had attacked him, decided not
to, as the farmer was not quite out of sight, and, calling
to Jumble, who had discreetly vanished on the farmer's
arrival and now came leaping out of the ditch, set off
along the road that had turned another bend and was
now spanning the world in the right direction. The rain
was beginning to fall, and William's spirits sank
somewhat. People had been jolly rotten to him so far,
driving him out of woods and throwing him out of fields.
He compared his lot with that of the hero of the book—
received with acclamation by the natives as he went
along, feasted and fêted. They gave him food, and bands
came and played under his window at night. Funny how
differently people were treating him, William.

A steady drizzle had set in. He plodded doggedly on
He was cold, tired and hungry. He seemed to have bee
walking for days and days. Funny he hadn't got to th
sea yet. England must be a jolly big island. He wa
almost tempted to regret having undertaken the adven
ture, but, having undertaken it, he was going to carry i
through. Besides, if he didn't, there'd be years and year
and years of those awful Wednesday afternoons wit
Miss Milton and being a tom-tit. A church clock slowl
struck four. Four. It *couldn't* be only four. He was s
hungry that if he didn't get something to eat soon he'
die of starvation. The road turned sharply to skirt
hedge that enclosed a house and garden. William stop
ped to consider the situation. He could skirt the hous
and garden like the road or he could go through th
hedge and make his way across the garden, trusting t
luck to get through safely. A convenient hole in th
hedge decided him. He'd go through the hedge an
make his way across the garden in a straight line. No on
seemed to be about. He'd just make a run for it if he me
anyone. If he kept on wasting time going round things
he'd never get round the world, and he didn't want t
take longer than he could help. He was jolly bored by i
already. He was having a much worse time than th
man in the book had had—knocked about by farmer
and chased out of woods and soaked with rain an
starved. . . .

He made his way through the hole in the hedge an
stood looking about him. The sky was grey and overcast
The rain was still falling. Even Jumble had lost his *joie
de-vivre* and was looking at William in a slightl
reproachful manner, as if asking why he didn't either d
something interesting or take him in out of the rain.

He made his way across the garden, passing a lon

French window that showed a cosy lighted room with a bright coal-fire and an old lady sitting at a table having her tea. It looked a good tea. There was toast and bread and butter and currant cake and chocolate biscuits. Hardly knowing what he was doing, William approached and stood there at the window, his nose flattened against the glass, his eyes fixed hungrily upon the dainties on which the old lady was feasting, while Jumble shivered disconsolately at his heels. Suddenly the old lady looked up and met his gaze. She didn't seem at all surprised. It might have been quite a usual thing to look up from her tea to find boys flattening their noses on her window watching her. She got up and, unfastening the catch of the glass door, threw it wide open.

"Come in, come in," she said. "My goodness, *aren't* you wet!"

"Yes, I am," agreed William, "but I don't mind bein' wet so much." For it had occurred to him that this was an excellent opportunity of starting the process of begging his way round the world. "I wonder—I don't want anythin' you're goin' to eat—but if you've got any crusts or things left over——"

"Oh, there's heaps more than I shall want, here," said the old lady. "You'd better join me."

She went over to a cupboard, took out a cup and saucer, and drew another chair up to the tea-table.

"Sit down there," she said. "You'll soon get warm. And your poor little dog can lie by the fire."

As if waiting for this permission, Jumble stretched himself out with a sigh of relief on the hearthrug and promptly fell asleep.

"There!" said the old lady, pouring out a cup of tea. "It's quite hot still and so is the toast."

"You see," explained William, somewhat taken

aback by this matter-of-fact reception and feeling that some explanation was called for, "I'm walkin' round the world with a dog. I'd rather've been ridin' round with two ponies, only I'd not got 'em—so I'm walkin' round with a dog."

"I know," said the old lady, nodding her head understandingly. "I used to play games like that, too."

"I DON'T WANT ANYTHIN' YOU'RE GOIN' TO EAT," SAID WILLIAM
"BUT IF YOU'VE GOT ANY CRUSTS LEFT OVER—"

William opened his mouth to explain, with something of indignation, that this was no game, but the old lady was handing him the toast and it seemed a pity to waste time in speech, so he took the toast and proceeded to make an extremely hearty meal. The rain lashed against

"OH, THERE'S HEAPS MORE THAN I SHALL WANT HERE," SAID THE OLD LADY.

the window. The sky grew darker. The prospect of spending the night under a hedge seemed less inviting than ever. . . .

"I was so glad to see you there at the window," said the old lady. "I was just saying to myself, 'I wish I'd got a boy to ask about it,' and then I looked up and saw you there. It seemed like Providence."

"Yes, it seemed like that to me, too," said William fervently.

"You see," went on the old lady, "I'm giving a party to some boys next Wednesday, and I really don't know the sort of thing they like. I want you to advise me." She took a piece of paper from a table near. "We'll make a list of food together when you've finished. And you can tell me the games you think they'd like, too."

William agreed through a mouthful of plum cake.

"You see," said the old lady again, still more confidentially, "it's because of my niece, really. She's been having a sort of class for boys on Wednesday afternoons. I don't quite know what it is, but they all have great fun and these boys love it. She's only been doing it for quite a short time, and now she's taken on the secretaryship of something or other and that means she'll have to give up these boys. Well, she's terribly disappointed, as you may imagine, at having to give it up. And, of course, the boys will be still more disappointed. In fact, she said that she didn't know how she was going to break it to them, so I suggested that she should have a party for them—just to cheer them up, you know—and as her house is rather small, I said she'd better have it here and that I'd arrange it all for her, because she's so very busy with this new work. What's the matter, dear?" for William was staring at her open-mouthed, everything else, even the chocolate biscuits, forgotten.

"W-w-w-what's her name?" he stammered.

"Miss Milton," said the old lady.

"An'—an'—an' is she goin' to have all these boys to the party?"

"Yes, dear, of course she is. Just to comfort them a little for having to give up these delightful classes. I thought it would be such a good idea. A little treat does so help to tide over a disappointment, doesn't it? She's going to go round to them all this evening and break the news to them and invite them to the party. So, if you've quite finished, dear, you can help me with the list."

Half an hour later William, warm and fed and comparatively dry, set off jauntily from the front door with Jumble at his heels. The rain had stopped, but William did not continue his course round the world. He had decided to abandon it for the present. There wouldn't be any sense in missing the party for which he had just drawn up such an adequate list of refreshments and entertainment. Besides, there wasn't much point in going away now that the hated Wednesday afternoons were coming to an end. What he'd tried of walking round the world he quite definitely hadn't enjoyed. Perhaps it would be better to wait till he was older and could get two ponies. Perhaps people would treat him a bit better if he was older and had two ponies, same as they did the man in the book. . . .

He had plenty of other plans in his mind. He'd like to have a shot at a boy sanctuary and charge admission and see if he couldn't make a bit of money that way. After all, it would be an awful waste of time taking five years walking round the world.

"Hurry up and get tidy, dear," said his mother as soon as he reached home. "Your tea's ready."

William entered the dining-room and looked with

dispassionate scorn at the plateful of bread and jam on the table. Nice fare that for a hero who'd just walked round the world! He bet the other man hadn't been given bread and jam when he got home. Still, he'd had quite a brisk walk since his tea with the old lady and, though he would have liked to show his scorn of the fare so unfit for a hero by refusing to partake of it, there was no doubt that bread and jam was better than nothing. He took a piece and bit into it. Mrs. Brown touched his shoulder tentatively.

"There, William!" she said reproachfully. "Your coat's quite damp. I do wish you'd be more careful. Surely you could have taken shelter during that shower."

"Huh!" ejaculated William significantly. "You can't bother about a little thing like rain when you're walkin' round the world. You're jolly lucky to have me back at all."

"What do you say, dear?" said Mrs. Brown absently.

William wondered whether to tell his mother of his heroic exploit (for by now he was almost convinced that he actually had walked round the world) but decided not to. She probably wouldn't listen to him and it would only be a waste of time.

As he reached out for another piece of bread and jam he saw the figure of Miss Milton coming up the drive. . . .

Chapter 9

Coronation Gala

CORONATION to the Outlaws meant at first merely an extra day's holiday, but as the day drew near they began to take an interest in it for its own sake. The local authorities at Hadley had decided to celebrate the event by a super Gala. Every year Hadley held a Gala in aid of its local charities—with decorated trade vans and prizes for fancy dress and swings and roundabouts and side-shows and competitions. This was to be the same sort of Gala, but larger, more impressive, more Gala-ish. It was to be held in a meadow just outside Hadley, and was to begin at 2.30 and go on till midnight, for there was to be dancing on a flood-lit piece of meadow as long as anyone was left to dance on it. It was, of course, in the shows and roundabouts that the Outlaws were particularly interested—and in the fancy dress. For everyone except the elderly and infirm was going in fancy dress.

Ginger was to wear a pirate costume, Douglas his tram conductor's set, and Henry a Dutch boy's costume that his aunt was lending him. William had not yet decided what he was to wear. Officially he was supposed to be wearing his Red Indian suit, but unofficially he had decided against it from the beginning. He was fond of it, but it was too ordinary, and everyone in the village knew it well—only too well—by sight. He wanted something new, something startling, something more suitable to the occasion than the old Red Indian suit. A coronation. He ought to go as a king. The more he thought about it the more determined he was to go as a king. After all, a king's costume was comparatively simple. It only needed a crown made out of a strip of cardboard, a paper fastener, and some gold paint, and a cloak that could generally be fashioned from a dressing gown or tablecloth. William would have been quite satisfied by this, had it not been for the magnificent king costume that Robert possessed. Robert was a member of the local dramatic society and had taken the part of the king in a play called *Cophetua and the Beggar Maid* that they had acted at Christmas. As well as the king costume, Robert possessed also a very fine "period" costume that he had worn in the *School for Scandal* the year before. William took a great interest in these costumes, but Robert guarded them closely and had never allowed him even to approach them.

So William set to work on the making of his king costume. He cut a strip of cardboard, painted it with gold paint and fastened it together with a paper fastener. It would have looked splendid if it hadn't been for the memory of Robert's crown, which had points and spikes and a jewel in the middle. His cloak was an old red kitchen tablecloth that his mother had let him have out of the rag-bag. It was folded crossways like a shawl and hung over his shoulders, fastened at the shoulders by pins. William tried to give the effect of an ermine border by sticking a strip of white paper along the edge and inking it at intervals, but it wasn't a success. The glue got everywhere and the ink got everywhere and the paper didn't stick straight, and so William abandoned the attempt, leaving the glue-and-ink-soaked paper tracing an erratic course for about a yard at the edge of the tablecloth.

"Which costume are you goin' to wear at the Gala, Robert?" he asked carelessly the next day.

"Mind your own business," said Robert, who liked William to know as little as possible of his affairs.

William, however, generally knew more about Robert's affairs than Robert suspected. Such knowledge might always come in useful, and in the eternal warfare waged between eleven and nineteen, eleven has need of all the resources it can muster.

William knew that Robert was at this time deeply attached to a local beauty of the name of Dahlia Macnamara. The lady was proud and haughty, and the affair had had many vicissitudes. Robert, in fact, had more than once washed his hands of the whole concern, forswearing women for ever and vowing himself to the life of an anchorite, but he had always returned to his allegiance on the faintest sign of encouragement from Dahlia. A little extra pep had been instilled recently into the affair by Robert's friend, Jameson Jameson, who had suddenly entered the lists for Dahlia's favour and, being something of a novelty, was treated by her with comparative graciousness. This naturally annoyed Robert, who was nothing of a novelty and who was treated with no graciousness at all. He refused, however, to yield the first place, and the two rivals (not for the first time in such circumstances) ran a neck-to-neck race. Robert had certain material advantages. Jameson did not belong to the dramatic club, and Dahlia was its star. Dahlia and Robert generally took the part of heroine and hero, while Jameson ground his teeth in the back row. It was Dahlia who had acted the beggar maid to Robert's King Cophetua. She had given quite a new conception to the character by endowing it with an air of extreme hauteur and disdain. Robert had, however, compensated for this by playing the king with the humility and diffidence usually associated with the beggar maid. The acting of both had been much praised in the local press (as, indeed, had the acting of everyone, for the local press set a fine example of impartiality and considered every member of the cast, duly mentioned in print, good for at least a dozen copies).

All this, then, William knew and kept tabulated at the back of his mind, though he didn't see how it could be utilised on the present occasion.

"I 'speck you're goin' in your king's costume, aren't you?" he went on.

"Never you mind what I'm going in," said Robert.

"I thought it looked a bit too small for you," said William nonchalantly. "The one you wore in the play, I mean."

"Oh, you did, did you?" said Robert sarcastically. "That's very interesting."

William abandoned attack from that quarter. He hadn't really expected Robert to believe that the costume was too small and promptly offer it to him, but he'd tried it on the principle that everything's worth trying once. He started attack from another quarter.

"I thought you looked jolly nice in that other costume," he went on. "That one with the wig an' lace collar an' suchlike. I've never seen you look as nice as you did in that one. I think you'd look jolly nice in that one at the Gala."

Robert did not deign to reply to this, and William's curiosity had to go unsatisfied for the moment, but only for the moment, for the next day he heard Robert telephoning to a friend and saying "The Gala? Oh, yes,

I'm going in my 'School for Scandal' costume. That'll be all right, won't it?"

William promptly laid his plans. Whatever happened he must have Robert's king costume—the lovely spiky, jewelled crown, the red robe with its beautiful border of inked cotton-wool. Robert wasn't going to wear it and, after all, it would be wrong for such a highly appropriate costume as that not to make its appearance at the Coronation. By the end of half an hour he had persuaded himself that it was his duty as a patriot to wear it. He did not, moreover, anticipate much difficulty in getting it. He knew exactly where it was. He would take it immediately before the Gala and restore it immediately after. And during the Gala he would carefully keep out of Robert's way. That, he thought, should not be difficult. His social circle and Robert's did not meet at any point, and, if he kept a look-out, it would be easy enough to avoid him.

The beginning of the plan worked quite well. Robert was out all the evening before the Gala, and William, on his way to bed, crept silently into his bedroom and took the costume from the middle drawer in Robert's chest of drawers where it was kept. There was a tunic and tights to wear beneath the robe, but William did not bother with them. They'd be too big, in any case, and he was not a stickler for details. He just took the crown and the robe. He took it out very carefully, leaving the drawer exactly as he had found it. He knew that the "School for Scandal" costume was in a cardboard box on the top of Robert's wardrobe and that there was nothing else in the middle drawer that Robert would be likely to want. Ever an optimist, he hoped for the best.

And at first his optimism seemed justified. The next morning at breakfast it was quite clear that Robert had not discovered his loss. He was jovial and in good spirits, said that he'd tried on the "School for Scandal" costume the night before and that it really was a jolly fine costume. He hinted that it was more than possible it might win a prize. He even chaffed William good-humouredly about the cardboard strip and the red tablecloth.

William, thinking that there was always a certain risk of discovery as long as the costume remained in his bedroom, conveyed it secretly to the old barn immediately after breakfast and tried it on before the admiring Outlaws. The cloak that just reached Robert's knees enveloped him completely, but the general effect was undoubtedly magnificent.

"I say!" said Ginger. "Let's have a coronation with it before the Gala. Same as they're doin' in London. The Gala doesn't start till half-past two so it'll be somethin' to do till then."

"All right," said William, "an' I'll be king."

They agreed to this. After all, it was William's costume and William was their leader.

"I'll be William the Conqueror," said William.

"You can't be," said Henry. "You've gotter be a new one. You'll have to be William the Fifth. 'Cause there's been four already."

"Well, I'm goin' to be William the Conqueror as well."

"You can't be," objected Henry.

The argument became a scuffle, then a wrestling match, then a free fight, in which everyone joined, and then it was time for lunch. All the Outlaws' families were having early lunch in order to give them time to change into Gala attire and get down to Hadley by half-past two. William went home somewhat apprehensively

prepared to dodge Robert's avenging hand with the skill
of long practice. But Robert was still placid and serene.
Evidently nothing had happened since breakfast. William, however, was wrong there. Though the loss of the
king costume had not yet been discovered, quite a lot
had happened since breakfast. For one thing Dahlia had
rung Robert up and suggested with unusual kindness
that they should go to the Gala together as King
Cophetua and the Beggar Maid.

"Wouldn't it be rather nice?" she said. "I'd simply
love it, wouldn't you? We did have such fun over that
play, didn't we?"

There was a lingering sweetness in the voice that went
to Robert's head. He stammered incoherent assent.

"I'd love to . . ." he said. "Simply *love* to. How
ripping of you to think of it. . . ."

"Were you going in that costume, anyway?"

"Yes . . . no . . . I don't know," stammered Robert.
"Of course, I am now. I say, it's ripping of you. I'm
terribly bucked about it. I——"

"That's all right, then," interrupted Dahlia, who
knew by experience that unless interrupted he would go
on for ever. "I'll be there at two-thirty or soon after."

Robert put down the receiver, wild-eyed with rapture.
She'd asked him to go with her as King Cophetua. She'd
asked him. *She'd* asked him. She'd asked *him*. Gosh! He
could hardly believe it. She'd rung him up and asked
him. Ha! It'd make that old Jameson look a bit small.
Putting on no end of airs, he'd been, lately, just because
Dahlia had rung him up once or twice. *This'd* show him
all right. Ha! Who had she asked to go with her to the
Gala? Who? *Who?* WHO? Or ought it to be whom? Not
that it mattered. He was going with Dahlia to the Gala as
King Cophetua and the Beggar Maid. Jameson Jameson

could put that in his pipe and smoke it. It would make
him even more sick than tobacco did. At this moment
Jameson Jameson appeared at the front door. He
looked nervous and ill-at-ease. Robert greeted him in a
genial patronising manner that would ordinarily have
annoyed Jameson extremely, but to-day Jameson,
despite his diffidence and humility, seemed preoccupied.

"I say, Robert," he began, "I hope you won't think it
awful cheek of me, but I was just sort of wondering
whether you could—I mean, if you aren't using it, of
course—I only wondered if you could lend me your
'School for Scandal' costume for the Gala, if you're not
using it, of course. It doesn't matter at all if you are. I
know you'd got some other costume and I only just
wondered if you were using that particular one. It's
awful cheek, of course."

Robert looked at him in silence, savouring the delicious irony of the situation. Here was Jameson trying to
borrow the "School for Scandal" costume in order,
presumably, to cut a dash in Dahlia's eyes, quite
unaware of the fact that Dahlia had already chosen
between them, had asked him, Robert, to accompany
her, to play King Cophetua to her Beggar Maid.
Triumph filled his heart—a vast benignity his eye.

"That's quite all right, Jameson," he said kindly.
"No, I wasn't going to wear that costume, and I'd be
very glad to lend it to you. I'll get it now."

He ran upstairs, lifted the cardboard box from the top
of his wardrobe and took it to the waiting Jameson. So
gleeful and triumphant was he feeling that it was all he
could do to hand it to Jameson with a straight face. As
soon as Jameson had disappeared, he danced a *pas seul*
of exultation on the doorstep as a slight outlet to his

eelings then went indoors for lunch. He did not bother
o get out his other costume because he took for granted
hat it was safely there in the middle drawer, and, of
ourse, he needn't start changing till after lunch.
3esides, he felt too much excited to do anything but
magine the scene at the Gala, when Jameson, all
dressed up in the "School for Scandal" costume, should
watch him and Dahlia strolling about together as King
Cophetua and the Beggar Maid.

He did not mention his change of plan at lunch. He did
not mention anything at lunch. He wasn't there at all.
He was with Dahlia at the Coronation Gala, wearing his
king costume, watched enviously and disconsolately by
Jameson Jameson decked out all unavailingly in his
borrowed plumes.

Immediately after lunch William made his way to the
old barn, where Ginger, Henry and Douglas were waiting for him. They had all entered fully into the spirit of
his coronation. Ginger had brought a wooden cart for
he coronation coach, Douglas had brought a poker and
a football for sceptre and orb, and Henry—ever well
informed—had brought some motor oil in a small tin
hat he had taken from the garage.

"You've gotter have it poured over you," he
explained to William. "They always do."

"*Me?*" said William indignantly. "That messy stuff. I
olly well won't."

"Then you won't be prop'ly crowned, that's all," said
Henry. "To be prop'ly crowned they've gotter have oil
poured over 'em."

"I bet the other one's not havin' it," said William,
referring to His Gracious Majesty, King George the
Sixth.

" 'Course he is," said Henry.

"I JOLLY WELL WON'T HAVE THAT MESSY STUFF POURED OVE[
ME."

"Stuff like that poured over his head?" said Willia[
incredulously, gazing at the thick viscous liquid.

" 'Course he is," said Henry.

There was something convincing in Henry's air o[
authority, and Ginger, too, said that he remembere[
reading in the paper that oil was poured over the Kin[
during the ceremony.

"THEN YOU WON'T BE PROP'LY CROWNED, THAT'S ALL," SAID
HENRY.

"Gosh!" said William amazed, and repeated, "Gosh!
No wonder people say it's no joke bein' a king . . ."

But, as he was taking the business seriously, he
decided to submit.

"All right," he went on, "but mind you don't make a

mess of this cloak thing of Robert's or I'll get in a row. He doesn't know I've taken it."

It was as well that William could not see Robert at that moment, turning the contents of all his drawers on to the floor in a frenzied search for the missing cloak and crown.

The ceremony in the barn proceeded. William was ensconced upon the packing-case that was its only piece of furniture, Henry poured the motor oil over his head to the accompaniment of a kingly yell of "Hi! that's enough! Don't go messin' all my things," Douglas mopped it off his head as best he could with his handkerchief, and Ginger solemnly placed the crown on it and said, "Rise, King William the Fifth."

"I bet that's not the way they really do it," said William, swallowing a trickle of motor oil that had somehow escaped Douglas's handkerchief. "Gosh! it does taste beastly. I'm jolly sorry for the other one if he's got as much of the stuff in his mouth as I have. Anyway, I'm king now and——"

"You've gotter drive back to the Palace first," interrupted Ginger importantly. "This is Westminster Abbey, an' you've gotter drive back to the Palace in your coach."

"All right," said William, who was beginning rather to resent the fashion in which he was being managed and organised. "All right. Then after that I'm goin' to start bein' a real king."

He got into the somewhat cramped wooden cart and was pushed and pulled round the field by the other three. He tried to imagine cheering crowds and bowed solemnly at intervals, but so bumpy was the field and so erratic the course steered by Ginger, Henry and Douglas that it was all he could do to keep his seat. They described a large circle and returned to the old barn.

"Now you're at your Palace," said Ginger.

"All right," said William. "Now I'm goin' to start bein' a real king. I've not had much fun so far—drinkin' oil an' bein' nearly bumped to death. What do they do nowadays—kings, I mean?"

"Oh, they jus' go about visitin' an' openin' things an' reviewin' troops an' tourin' places."

"Well, I'm not goin' to be one of those," said William firmly. "I'm goin' to be the sort they had in hist'ry what put down rebels an' suchlike."

"There aren't any rebels, nowadays," said Henry.

"I bet there are. Nat'rally they don't go about *sayin'* they're rebels. I bet I could find some if I started lookin' for 'em. Stands to reason there mus' be some. People jus' don't bother. lookin' for 'em, an' then, when a rebellion breaks out, it'll be too late. I'm goin' to find 'em now I'm king an' put 'em down."

They looked at him somewhat apprehensively. William never seemed to know when imagination ended and reality began.

The village clock struck two.

"Time we went down to Hadley, anyway," said Ginger, torn between relief and disappointment, for William's rebel hunt would probably have been quite exciting.

A stream of people, mostly in fancy dress, could be seen walking down the road to Hadley.

"I can't go by the road," said William. "I'll have to go the long way by the fields 'cause I don't want to meet Robert. He doesn't know I've got his things."

At this moment a desperate wild-eyed Robert was searching William's bedroom for the missing costume. He had on the tunic and the long stockings, but what were they without the cloak and crown? In William's wardrobe he found the cardboard crown and the red tablecloth. It was easy enough to see what had happened. The little devil had started making a costume of his own, given up the attempt in despair, and pinched his, Robert's.

"Wait till I get hold of him," he muttered fiercely. "Just wait till I get hold of him."

But his lust for vengeance would have to be curbed for the present. Time was getting on, and his beggar maid would be waiting for him at the entrance of the Gala ground unless he hurried. Dahlia kept waiting was something at which the imagination boggled. The clock was striking two. He must go down to Hadley at once and he must go as a king. His beggar maid would never forgive him if he didn't. Gritting his teeth ("Wait till I get hold of him! Just *wait*!"), he put on the cardboard crown and, savagely tearing off William's unsuccessful attempts at ermine, draped the red tablecloth over his shoulder, then, slamming the door, set off for Hadley.

William and the Outlaws entered Hadley by the field-path that led into a lane and thence into a maze of back streets. The back streets were mostly deserted, for the population of Hadley was already on the Gala meadow or lining the main streets which were the route of the procession of decorated trade vans.

"Come on," said Ginger. "Let's go'n' watch the procession."

"No, let's go straight to the meadow," said Henry, "an' have a go on the roundabout an' things before all the others get to 'em."

"I'm not doin' either," said William. "I'm goin' to look for rebels. I bet this is jus' the time they'd choose to meet. There's no one about, an' all the policemen are in the procession streets keepin' the crowds back. It's jus' the time for rebels to come out an' fix things up together. Well, I bet I would if I was a rebel, anyway."

"Oh, come on," said Douglas. "I tell you there *aren't* any rebels."

"All right," said William. "You an' Henry go to the Gala, an' Ginger an' me'll stop here an' look for rebels an' I bet you anythin' you like we'll find some."

"Very well," agreed Douglas, "but"—anxiously (for William's attitude as usual carried conviction)—"you'll fetch us if you do find any, won't you? We'll keep near the gate."

"Yes," promised William. "It'd be best to split up, anyway, 'cause we don't want 'em to get suspicious with a lot of us lookin' for 'em. It'd put 'em on their guard, seein' all four of us. You an' Henry go to the meadow an' I'll send Ginger to fetch you soon as we catch any. It'd be rather nice"—wistfully—"to bring 'em along in chains at the end of the procession, but we've not got any chains."

Henry and Douglas set off for the meadow, and William and Ginger began to walk through the deserted back streets. A few belated trades vans, decked out for the Gala, passed them. Outside a public-house stood a small deserted trade van inscribed with "G. Perkins, Butcher", hung with red, white and blue bunting and with a little island of potted palms in the middle. At the corner of the public-house stood a group of men lounging against the wall. As William and Ginger appeared, they were passing slips of paper furtively to another man who vanished as soon as he'd received them.

William hastily drew Ginger aside.

"Rebels," he said excitedly. "Din't you see?"

"What?" said Ginger.

"Those bits of paper. They were plans an' things. Maps tellin' 'em where to meet and where to start the rebellion. Well, you could see they were rebels, cun't you? They *looked* like rebels. Let's walk past an' listen to what they're saying'. Come on."

They strolled slowly past the group again. One large burly man with a bulbous nose and stubbly chin seeming to be the centre. He looked at Ginger and Douglas and spat contemptuously, then continued the conversation.

"I've allus fancied Republic," he was saying.

William grabbed Ginger's arm and drew him aside again.

"Did you hear?" he whispered. "He is a rebel. He wants a republic. 'Course he's a rebel. Din't I tell you? Let's go back an' hear some more."

They strolled past the group again. The large burly man was talking about "ten to one" and "ran in the Newmarket Stakes".

"There, you see," said Ginger, when they were out of earshot again. "It's only racin' they're talkin' about."

"Ah," said William with an air of deep wisdom. "They pretended it was only racin' as soon as they saw we were listenin'. He gave 'em a sign an' they all started pretendin' it was racin'. I 'spect they always do that when they see someone listenin'."

The group was dispersing. The large burly man and a very thin one in a voluminous belted check overcoat that would have taken four of him climbed up into the driving-seat of the lorry and sat there talking in undertones.

"I'm goin' to get up to listen to 'em," said William. "I bet they're talkin' about plans for the rebellion. You go'n' tell Douglas an' Henry that we've found 'em

Shun't be surprised if they've got a bomb an' are goin' to blow up the Gala."

The street was now deserted except for the stationary van and the two men in the driver's seat. William began to clamber up on to the van.

"I say!" gasped Ginger. "Had you better?"

"Go on quick an' tell Douglas an' Henry," said William.

He was now on the lorry just behind the driving-seat concealed by a piece of blue bunting.

"I *say*!" expostulated Ginger again, but the lorry started with a lurch that precipitated William into the island of potted palms. He sat up, rubbed his head, replaced his crown, straightened the disarranged island, waved his hand to Ginger in a gesture that might have been farewell, triumph or exhortation, and disappeared from view round the bend of the road.

Ginger set off hurriedly towards the meadow.

William made his way back to the point of vantage just behind the driving-seat, but it was a somewhat difficult post, for not only did the noise of the engine completely drown any conversation that might be taking place between the two men, but the frequent lurches of the lorry sent him down each time into the island of potted palms. Finally he decided to stay there. Perhaps the engine might get quieter later on. Anyway, he was tired of being jolted about, and, though there was no one to watch him, he could pretend that the deserted streets were lined with cheering crowds. There was something of dignity about it that Ginger's handcart had lacked. He was the king returning from Westminster Abbey to his Palace. Seated on a potted palm, he bowed gravely and with great dignity at intervals to an imaginary cheering multitude. The lorry wheeled suddenly into the main street and took its place at the tail-end of the procession of decorated tradesmen's vehicles.

The main street actually was crowded with a cheering multitude, but to William it was hardly more real than the imaginary crowds he had bowed to in the empty side street. He continued to sit on the plant-pot in the centre of the cart and to bow gravely at intervals. The procession entered the gates of the meadow and drove slowly past the platform on which were assembled the group of local dignitaries. The blare of the roundabout and shouts of merrymakers echoed on all sides. William was so immersed in his kingly role that he was oblivious of everything else, till suddenly something brought him abruptly to earth. Across the heads of the crowd he met Robert's eye, an angry accusing eye, an eye that gleamed with the anticipatory joy of vengeance . . . Robert, wearing the discarded cardboard crown with the red tablecloth draped across his shoulders.

Robert, running all the way from the village to Hadley, had arrived at the trysting-place just in time. And there he had his first shock. For Dahlia's costume was far from suggesting that of any beggar maid. The dress (of silver lamé) that she had worn for the part in the play had been freely criticised by the unsympathetic, but this was of flowered silk, made in a Gainsborough fashion, completed by a white curled wig and an enormous picture hat. She looked at Robert coldly.

"What on earth's that you've got on your shoulders?" she said.

"It's my cloak," said Robert, also a little coldly. "I couldn't find the other. It had got mislaid."

Her glance wandered to his crown.

"And that," she said. "What do you think this is? A kindergarten end-of-term party? Did you get it out of a cracker or find it in a bran-tub? You evidently don't consider me worth taking much trouble over."

Robert had meant to tell her the whole story and let her apply the balm of womanly sympathy to his wounds, but her tone irritated him.

"Come to that," he said, looking at her, "you're not so much like a beggar maid yourself."

She tossed the elaborately wigged and hatted head.

"How *dare* you insult me?" she said dramatically.

"I'm not insulting you," said Robert, sticking to his guns. "I'm only saying that no beggar maid ever had clothes like those."

"And if you think any king ever had clothes like *those*," said Dahlia, with withering sarcasm, "I'm sorry for you. I don't see why I should stoop to justify myself to you, but, naturally, I'm dressed as the beggar maid *after* she married the king, not before. If you think I'm going to trail about in rags to please you you're very much mistaken."

"I don't imagine that you'd do anything to please me," said Robert, wavering between pathos and hauteur.

"Oh, don't you?" said Dahlia with another toss of her head. "Well, let me tell you not many girls would be seen out with such a figure of fun as you are."

"Figure of *fun*?" said Robert. "I like that. I—I say," pathos triumphing over hauteur, "don't let's quarrel. Let's—er—go and have a look round, shall we?"

They wandered round the meadow, Robert keeping a stern look-out for William. If he came upon the wretched kid wearing his things, nothing in the world would stop him executing vengeance on him then and there. Dahlia was preoccupied, ignoring all Robert's efforts at friendly conversation.

"YOU'RE NOT SO MUCH LIKE A BEGGAR MAID YOURSELF."
"HOW DARE YOU INSULT ME!" SHE SAID DRAMATICALLY.

"Let's have a go at the coconuts, shall we?" said
Robert at last.

Robert was rather good at coconut shies and hoped to
restore his prestige in Dahlia's eyes by his prowess.

"All right," said Dahlia without much interest.

They went to the coconut shy, and Robert paid for six balls. He flung them one after the other with much arm-play and increasing self-confidence. One coconut—two—three. Three coconuts for six balls. It wasn't bad. She'd feel a bit different about him now probably. He turned with a complacent smile to receive her congratu-altions, and—she wasn't there. The complacent smile died from his lips and his mouth dropped open. She'd gone. She'd calmly sloped off and left him. The whole thing was like a nightmare. That wretched kid pinching his costume and then Dahlia calmly sloping off and leaving him. He made his way through the crowds to look for her. Then he saw her in the distance. She was with Jameson—Jameson resplendent in his "School for Scandal" costume.

He went towards them, but somehow they evaded him and he was left alone again. He set off to find them again, and again they evaded him. It was clear that they were deliberately keeping out of his way. In the fugitive glimpses he had of them they were laughing and talking together with a friendliness that increased Robert's rage. All Dahlia's hauteur and languor were gone. She was smiling up at Jameson, and Jameson was beaming down on her, looking more like a half-witted jackass than ever, thought Robert savagely. And their costumes went well together. He couldn't help realising that. They might have decided to go together as an eighteenth-century couple. And suddenly a dreadful suspicion smote Robert. Perhaps they *had* decided to go together as an eighteenth-century couple. Perhaps it was all a deep-laid plot. Perhaps she'd rung him up to ask him to go out with her as King Cophetua and the Beggar Maid, simply to ensure his lending the other costume to

Jameson, and had meant all the time to give him the slip and join his rival.

Grinding his teeth with fury, Robert plunged desperately through the crowd. People he pushed against made depreciatory remarks about his tablecloth and cardboard crown. That brought him back to the source of all the trouble. It was that wretched kid who was at the bottom of it all. Wait till he got hold of him. Just *wait* . . . The crowd surged towards the entrance gate of the meadow. The procession of decorated vans was just coming in. Robert was carried with it willynilly and stood wedged in between a fat woman with a shopping basket and a thin clown whose colour was coming off in trickles of perspiration. The trades vans drove slowly by. Robert wasn't interested in them. They all had the same scheme of decoration every year, and the same three always got the prize. This year there were red, white and blue hangings and a sprinkling of Union Jacks, but otherwise it was just the same as last year and the year before. The tradesmen of Hadley were a conservative lot.

Sunk in gloomy thought, Robert watched them pass, laden with their decorated wares, for each competitor was more interested in advertising his merchandise than in signalising the occasion. A dining-room suite swathed in bunting, water softeners crowned by Union Jacks, mountainous slabs of imitation butter and cheese wreathed in faded roses, mannequins wearing the latest (Hadley) fashions, with red, white and blue ribbons in their hair. . . . And then came a small cart with hangings of bunting, a group of potted palms in the middle, and, sitting in the very centre of the potted palms, a well-known figure resplendent in robe and crown. Robert tried to fight his way through the crowd to get at that figure and deal out instant vengeance, but the crowd was too thick. However—the little wretch would have to get down off that cart sometime, and Robert didn't mean to let him out of his sight till he had got down and then . . . Oh, just wait!

All the humiliation of the afternoon originated in the little wretch. If he'd been able to wear his own crown and robe he might even now be wandering with a smiling admiring Dahlia among the coconut shies and side shows, for the suspicion that Dahlia and Jameson had hatched a deep plot to dispense with him and disport themselves together in eighteenth-century costume was too horrible to be entertained for more than a moment. He began to force his way through the crowd, keeping alongside the cart, fixing a grim menacing eye on William. William, his dreams of kingly progress abruptly shattered, looked round hurriedly for some way of escape. But the only way of escape seemed to be to stay where he was. To jump down from the cart into the crowd would be to deliver himself completely into Robert's hands. So he sat there, between the devil of Robert's vengeance and the deep sea of his unknown driver, ready to make a desperate bolt for safety the minute his presence on the cart was discovered and he was, as he presumably would be, unceremoniously ejected. But the lorries and vans and carts had come to a stop.

The Mayor was making a speech from the platform and adjudicating the prizes. The Mayor was a little disappointed in the tradesmen of Hadley. There had been no fundamental changes in the design of their decorations for the last three or four years. Even this unique occasion—the Coronation of their King—had inspired nothing but the addition of a few flags and

tricoloured ribbons. All but one. And he had to congratulate that one on the boldness of his conception and
the originality of his design. Mr. Perkins had conceived
the idea of a tableau of a boy king, an idea that both
commemorated the unique historic event of the day and
linked with it the idea of youth, the inheritor of the vast
empire whose king was even now being crowned at
Westminster. It was a touching idea, a patriotic idea, an
idea that showed a deep sense of spiritual values. (It was
at this point that the bewildered Mr. Perkins got down
from his driver's seat and saw his strange cargo for the
first time.) William, meantime, remained seated on his
potted palm, his face set and inscrutable, his eyes fixed
warily on Robert, ready to anticipate the slightest movement on his part.

The Mayor had great pleasure in awarding the first
prize to Mr. Perkins. Other vans were, he knew, more
elaborately dressed, but this was the only one that had
conceived an entirely fresh scheme of decoration to
meet the spirit of the occasion. Mr. Perkins, still scratch-
ing his head and gazing in a fascinated manner at
William, went forward to receive his prize. The other
prizes were presented. The crowd began to melt away.
The moment had come when William must give an
account of himself to someone. . . . Mr. Perkins was
approaching his cart. Despite his 1st prize (a large
certificate printed in gold letters), he wore the expression of a man who has been made a fool of and is going to
know the reason why. Just by the lorry waited Robert,
his mouth set, in his eye that look of grim determination
that William knew only too well. And then, as if by a
miracle, William was saved.

Someone was helping him down from the cart and
presenting him to the Member of Parliament for Hadley

and his wife. They shook hands with him and complimented him on his crown, robe, and the tableau generally.

"You must be proud of helping to win the first prize," said the Member's wife.

"Are you Mr. Perkins's son?" said the Member.

"No, not exactly," said William.

He dragged out an account of his name and age to an exorbitant length, frequently giving the same information several times over, aware all the time of Robert waiting like an inexorable figure of fate about a yard away. The Member and his wife lived in London and bore the air of a larger and more fashionable world than Hadley. Even Robert would not dare to attack him in their presence. He was telling them his age for the fifth time and was just going to tell them his name for the sixth and they were obviously waiting an opportunity of bringing the interview to an end when suddenly an idea struck William. He delivered a master stroke. He turned to the waiting spectre of vengeance that was Robert and said:

"This is my brother. He very kindly lent me his things, else I couldn't have done it."

Amazement, indignation, fury chased themselves over Robert's features, which, however, had perforce to settle into a polite smile as the Member and his wife shook hands with him and congratulated him.

"That was very kind of you," they said.

"Not at all," murmured Robert.

"He very kindly wore mine so's I could wear his for this tableau thing," went on William.

"How very kind!" murmured the Member and his wife again.

"Would you like to change back now, Robert?" went

WILLIAM TURNED TO THE VENGEFUL ROBERT. "THIS IS MY
BROTHER. HE VERY KINDLY LENT ME HIS THINGS, ELSE I COULDN'T
HAVE DONE IT."

on William. "Thank you awfully for letting me have
them."

Robert could do nothing but murmur acquiescence.
He handed over the tablecloth and cardboard crown and

ROBERT WAS SPEECHLESS WITH AMAZEMENT AND INDIGNATION.

put on his own robe and crown in return. Obviously, however, the Member and his wife, unlike William, considered the possibilities of the situation to be exhausted and were already turning away, though William was just beginning to tell them his age again, when a girl came up and joined them.

"Hello, Mummy," she said and smiled at William. "Is that the boy on the cart?"

"Yes, dear," said her mother, "and this is his brother who kindly lent him this costume."

"What a kind brother!" said the girl, smiling at Robert. "Mine never lends me anything."

Robert gazed at her, tongue-tied and blushing. She was the loveliest girl he'd ever seen in his life. She knocked Dahlia Macnamara into the middle of next week. And even Robert could tell that her clothes were smarter than those of any other girl for miles around. She looked like the sort of girl you see on the pictures.

"Isn't it dreadful?" she went on to Robert. "I simply don't know a soul here. It shows what a bad M.P.'s daughter I am, doesn't it?"

"Won't you come round with me," said Robert, his tongue suddenly coming untied, "and see all the sights?"

"Oh, I'd love to," she said. "What fun!"

They set off together. They passed Jameson and Dahlia. The girl was just laughing at something Robert had said. Robert did not apparently notice Jameson and Dahlia. Dahlia gazed at him, horror-stricken, outraged, then turned to snap off Jameson's unoffending head.

William hurried through the crowd in search of his Outlaws. He'd decided not to bother any more about rebels or kings or coronations. He'd had a tiring afternoon and he thought he'd like a nice rest on the roundabouts or helter-skelter or wild sea waves.

Chapter 10

William and the Love Test

WILLIAM had, not for the first time, become deeply interested in the love affairs of his sister Ethel. Ethel was a young lady of unusual attractions, and her love affairs were naturally, therefore, of a somewhat kaleidoscopic nature. Most of the youths of the neighbourhood had at one time or another been so deeply enamoured of her that the only boon they had craved of life was to die rescuing her from fire or an enraged bull or a gang of kidnappers. They generally recovered, but were always liable to a second or even third or fourth attack of this malady. Her present most fervent admirers were two youths who had only recently come to the neighbourhood, and that was why William, bored by the local brand of Ethel's admirers, had suddenly become interested. The names of the new admirers were Richard and Charles—Ethel's admirers never seemed to have surnames—and they were both important figures at the local tennis club. Richard was large and muscular and wore the air of a strong silent man when he happened to be silent, which was very seldom, and Charles was tall and lithe and wiry with carefully cherished side-whiskers. They subjected Ethel to a ceaseless rain of chocolates and flowers—a process of which Ethel,

inured to it as she was, could never grow weary. She
received their offerings with the smile and dimples that
had made her famous throughout the countryside, went
for walks with them, danced with them, played tennis
with them, and drove with them in their small but
colourful sports cars. They seemed to run a neck-to-neck
race for her favour, and Jimmie Moore, her chronic local
admirer, was completely ousted. William rather liked
Jimmie, but Jimmie had long since passed the stage of
considering it necessary to propitiate William by occasional half-crowns, had learnt, indeed, that a William
interested in the progress of his love affair with Ethel
was more dangerous than a William alienated or indifferent. Richard and Charles were still at the stage of
slipping an occasional coin into William's hand and
looking at him through something of the glamour that
hung about the Beloved.

"Such a dear little boy," murmured Charles, caress-
ing his side-whiskers.

"Nice little fellow, isn't he?" said Richard heartily.

William made the most of this state of affairs, aware
that it never lasted long and that Ethel herself did little to
encourage it. Excitement rose high, however, among
those interested in the situation when the day of the
Tennis Club Annual Tournament drew near. For there
was to be a dance in the evening, and both Charles and
Richard had asked Ethel to attend the dance as his
partner. Ethel, with an adroitness of which she was past
mistress, put off the final decision.

"Is it to be me or that ass with fungus on his cheeks?"
demanded Richard belligerently.

"You're coming with me, aren't you?" said Charles.
"Richard can't dance for nuts, you know. Those fat men
never can."

"He's not exactly fat," murmured Ethel, "and he dances quite nicely."

"If you go with him I'll blow my brains out," said Charles.

But as Richard had said that he would drown himself if she went with Charles, this left the situation exactly where it was before.

When Ethel repeated to each the tragic threat of the other, Charles said that Richard was too fat to sink, and Richard said that Charles hadn't any brains to blow out.

"Don't hurry me so," remonstrated Ethel to each of them as they pleaded their cause. "I can't make up my mind about an important thing like that all in a second."

William's attitude was strictly impartial. Each of them had slipped a half-crown into his hand, murmuring as he did so a hope Ethel would go to the dance with him. Even to William their faith in his influence over Ethel was a little pathetic. Still—though not able exactly to influence Ethel, he often could and did influence a situation, and he was watching this one carefully. Jimmie, too, had asked Ethel to go to the dance as his partner, but Ethel was so used to Jimmie that she hadn't even considered it necessary to answer his letter. And he hadn't given William a half-crown or even a halfpenny, so that William, too, ruled him completely out of the situation.

As a situation it was, from Ethel's point of view, eminently satisfactory, but the decision could not be put off indefinitely. Delightful as the prospect was, she could not let them come to actual blows for her favour on the night of the dance. Public opinion would, she was aware, be against her if she did so.

"Well, darling," said Doris Clarke, her girl friend of the moment, "which are you going to the dance with?"

"WELL, DARLING," SAID DORIS, "WHICH OF THEM ARE YOU
GOING TO THE DANCE WITH?"

Doris, being temporarily without a love affair of her
own, was passionately interested in Ethel's.

Ethel drew her perfect brows together and sighed.

"I really don't know," she said. "I simply can't make
up my mind."

William was in the room, listening. He remembered

suddenly that he had once stayed with an aunt whose housemaid had been similarly troubled by two persistent suitors, between whose claims her heart was unable to judge. He remembered the means she had chosen to assist her in the decision.

"Have a test between them Ethel," he said.

Ethel, who had not known that he was there, looked at him coldly.

"Who asked you to chip in?" she said and added, yielding to her curiosity: "What sort of a test?"

William remembered that the actual test arranged by his aunt's housemaid had not been very successful. But he remembered, too, the magazine story from which she had taken the idea.

"Pretend you've lost all your money," he suggested, "and see which of them sticks to you."

"Don't be silly;" she said curtly. "I haven't any money to lose. Only three and six anyway. And in any case we don't want *your* opinion, thanks very much, so you can clear out and not sit listening to conversations that aren't meant for you."

William, aware that however long the argument lasted it would end in his sister's victory, forebore to argue. Instead, he went from the room with slow dignity, wondering, not for the first time, what people saw in Ethel, and wishing that they could have her for a sister for a bit, which, he decided, would jolly well *learn* them.

But, despite Ethel's pretended scorn, the thought of a test rather intrigued her.

"I think I *will* try to think of a test," she said after the door had shut on William's dignified and reluctant form. "I won't tell William anything about it, but if I can think of a good one, it *would* simplify matters."

"And I'll think, too, darling," said Doris, thrilled to

the core by the romantic idea, "and we'll meet to-
morrow and compare notes, shall us?"

They met the next day to compare notes. Doris first
suggested that Ethel should shave her eyebrows completely and cut off her hair close to her head and see
which of the two suitors still loved her thus disfigured.
Ethel received this suggestion coldly. Next, Doris suggested that Ethel should go to the tennis tournament
wearing clothes selected from the "jumble" that was
stored in Mrs. Brown's attic in readiness for the rum-
mage-sale and see which of them would then wish to be
her escort. This suggestion, too, Ethel received coldly.
Nothing daunted, Doris next suggested that Ethel
should pretend to be drunk at the tennis tournament and
see which of them continued to love her thus publicly
disgraced. Ethel's coldness deepened in intensity.

"I don't think it's any use you making any more
suggestions, dear," she said distantly. "You don't seem
to understand the situation at all. I shall have to think of
something by myself."

So she thought of something by herself. It was on the
whole quite a good idea. She decided to send each of
them a note on the day of the tournament, saying that
she had a headache, and asking each to come and sit with
her instead of playing in the tournament. For she knew
that to each of them the winning of the Men's Singles
Championship was the summit of his earthly ambitions.
For weeks past each had been feverishly practising,
frenziedly counting his chances, jealously watching the
other's progress. There was no one else in the running at
all. And, therefore, Ethel reasoned, it would be a real
test of love to give up this cherished chance of glory in
order to sit with her and soothe her (presumably) aching
brow.

This idea was communicated to Doris, who thought it excellent. Doris had been restored to favour on acknowledging that her suggestions had been quite impracticable. "And in any case, darling," she had added tactfully, "they wouldn't really have been *tests* at all. I mean, whatever you wore and whatever you did you'd still be *adorable*.

"Yes, yours is really romantic," she went on, "I mean, it's *really* romantic. Well, I mean whichever does it must really love you. I mean, *really* love you."

Doris was a well-intentioned girl, but she seemed to think that no statement was complete until it had been repeated several times in the same or different words. This gift of hers for serving up the same statement in any number of different ways amounted, indeed, almost to genius.

"You see," she went on earnestly. "Well, what I mean to say is that if they'd give up the chance of the championship—well, it *shows*, doesn't it? I mean, they wouldn't do it unless they loved you, would they? I mean, it *does* prove they love you, doesn't it! Well, I do think it does. I mean, if they'd give up a chance like that, it shows they love you better than a chance like that, and—well, it *does* show they love you, doesn't it? You see——"

"Yes," interrupted Ethel. "Now let's think about the letters."

The letters when finally written were short and to the purpose—shorter and more to the purpose than Doris approved of.

DEAR RICHARD [the other, of course, Dear Charles],
    I have rather a headache this afternoon and am not coming to the tournament, so would like you to

come and keep me company. Don't bother to send an
answer but if you aren't here by three I shall know you
aren't coming.

Yours,
ETHEL BROWN.

"I'd say a bit more than that, I would really," pleaded
Doris. "I mean, why don't you say something about how
it proves their love for you to give up a chance of honour
and glory like that. I really would say something about
that if I were you. I *really* would. I'd say that—well, that
if they can give up a chance of honour and glory like that
it will show you that they love you."

"No," said Ethel shortly, "I don't want them to know
it's a test, and you must promise not to breathe a word to
William."

Doris promised at great length not to breathe a word
to William, and kept her promise, but as it happened
William did find out about it. Rummaging on Ethel's
desk for some paper to make into a paper boat, he came
across the two notes. At first it merely seemed odd to
him that Ethel had written to both of them, then the still
odder fact struck him that the notes were dated for a
week ahead—the day of the tournament. Then suddenly
he understood. It was the test. And he felt the natural
righteous indignation of the artist on discovering that his
idea had been plagiarised and inadequately carried out
by the plagiarist. What a rotten test! He could have
thought of something much better than that with his eyes
shut. He *had* indeed thought of something much better.
He knew, however, that it would be useless to suggest it
to Ethel. He must just keep it to himself and have it
ready in case of need. Considering that the test was his
idea in the first place, he thought that Ethel might have

consulted him about it. However, he'd be generous and still help her.

The day of the tournament arrived. The notes were sent. Ethel sat in the drawing-room, trying to maintain an expression of suffering, and anxiously awaiting the result of her experiment. It would be awful if neither of them came. She had refused to allow Doris to be with her, though Doris had pleaded earnestly and at great length.

It was nearly three now, and neither had come yet, but she had purposely sent the notes late, so that they would have no chance of communicating with each other.

In order to reach the Browns' house, each suitor must cross a safe but narrow bridge, spanning a lake that had originally been a quarry but was now disused and full of water. William stood on the bridge with a hat of Ethel's concealed beneath his coat. He stood at a point from which he could see the field path by which the suitor—or suitors—must come. And suddenly he saw them striding along in silence, side by side, neck to neck, their faces stern and grim. Each had set out immediately on receiving the note. They had met on the way without greeting and, without resorting to the indignity of running, each was trying to outpace the other. A rotten test, thought William, watching them dispassionately.

Suddenly with a quick movement of his arm he threw Ethel's hat down from the bridge into the water, then stood there waving his arms wildly and shouting "Help!" to the oncoming youths. They quickened their pace to a run. "Hi!" shouted William, pointing to the hat, "Ethel's fallen into the lake."

That would be a test all right. He'd see which dived in to save her. Even if they both dived in he'd see which dived in first.

As one man they flung off their coats and dived in from the parapet of the bridge. Side by side they dived, without an inch to choose between them.

Bother them! thought William. Well, anyway, he would see which went on longest trying to save her. . . . They rose to the surface as one man. Together they shouted:

"Where did she go in?"

WILLIAM STOOD WAVING HIS ARMS AND SHOUTING TO THE ONCOMING YOUTHS.

THEY QUICKENED THEIR PACE TO A RUN. "HI!" SHOUTED
WILLIAM, "ETHEL'S FALLEN IN."

William once more pointed vaguely to the water
"There!" he said. "Somewhere about where her ha
is."

They dived and redived, they searched the ledges o
the quarry under the water, they arose dripping ever
now and then to shout questions at William. At last the
climbed out at the further side of the lake and sat
panting and dripping, on a stone ledge, too exhauste
even to shout further questions at William.

And then—a strange and unexpected sight met thei
gaze. Across the bridge came Ethel, dainty and immacu
late, accompanied by Jimmie Moore. She had waited til
after three o'clock, and then had decided with mucl
chagrin that both her suitors had failed in the test. At an
rate, she thought angrily, she wasn't going to sit there
waiting for them any longer. It was just when she ha
come to that decision that Jimmie Moore had arrived t
ask if she would come to the tournament with him. H
had already written to this effect and, as usual, ha
received no answer, but he had a fund of quiet per
sistence that made him not quite so negligible a rival a
Richard and Charles had believed.

"Yes, I'd love to," said Ethel, smiling on hin
sweetly. "I'll put on my hat and come at once."

She didn't want those wretches to think she'd bee
waiting for them. . . . Her anger had made her eyes ver
bright and her cheeks were pink, and she looke
extremely pretty.

"Where are Richard and Charles?" said Jim.

"Richard and Charles?" said Ethel as if puzzled
then, as if remembering suddenly something so unim
portant that she had almost forgotten it: "Oh, thos
two! I've really no idea. Playing in the tournament,
suppose. I'm afraid I'm not in the least interested"—sh

not him her ravishing smile—"are you?"

He grinned at her.

"You bet your life I'm not," he said.

They had come to the bridge, and there they found William leaning over the parapet staring fixedly at the water.

"What are you looking at?" said Jimmie.

"I thought I saw a trout," said William.

He said the first thing that came into his head, knowing that Jimmie as a fisherman would be interested.

For a moment the three of them stood looking down into the water. William was acutely aware of two dripping, panting figures on the other side of the lake, speechless with water and indignation, gazing in wild amazement at their three backs. As the other two moved away he said "There!" pointing excitedly at the water again.

As long as he could keep the attention of Ethel and her swain concentrated on the side of the bridge away from those two dripping, speechless, furious figures, the awkward moment might still be tided over.

"Come along," said Ethel impatiently, "we shall be late."

"May I come with you Ethel?" said William with an air of disarming meekness.

If he was with Ethel the vengeance that those dripping figures represented would at any rate be postponed.

"All right," said Ethel, without much enthusiasm.

They passed on, William still pointing out the mythical trout every now and then in order to keep Ethel's head turned away from her still speechless rescuers.

Just as they passed out of sight William glanced back.

Richard and Charles still sat side by side on the rock, two human rivulets gasping out water and fury and bewilderment and threats of vengeance to come.

He edged nearer to his unconscious defenders.

"Oh, well," he said, uttering his thoughts aloud, "it doesn't matter, and anyway it was a jolly good test, even if it didn't quite come off."

"What on earth are you talking about, William?" said Ethel impatiently.

"Nothin'," replied William.

THE END